The Caged Ruby

The Caged Ruby

Yellow Fever Series Book 1

Rodney Syler

Published by Tablo

I dedicate this book to my dad, Roy Clayton Syler, who passed away this year at ninety three years of age. He encouraged me, believed in me and I never wanted to let him down. That is probably a big reason I believed in myself. Bits and pieces of his sage advice pop up in these books as good lessons in life. He encouraged us to leave things a little better than we found them. He helped others without fanfare or need for recognition. He thought before he spoke and his word and a handshake was enough. I hope I can pass on some of his wisdom and goodness in these stories.

Chapter 1

Late in the evening as Taylor organized the parts in her dad's garage, a shoe crashed through the small window in the door to the house. Bits of glass tinkled to the floor as she moved her arms from over her head and reached to turn the music up a notch. Picking the shoe from the floor, she sat it neatly on the step, swept the glass, and resumed straightening the garage. She kept a radio at mid-volume, not because of the music, but to avoid hearing the raised voices in the house.

Lately her father spent more time trying to keep her mom calm, and less time teaching Taylor about cars. It was not a total loss. She could learn most everything on her own. If it was in books, she could learn it instantly. What she craved was to learn what people knew that was not in the books. The feelings and intuition, the facial expressions that gave weight to words, these things could only be learned face to face. She missed the face to face time with both her mom and dad.

Her dad was a race car mechanic and builder. He was not the best driver, but he knew more about tuning a car to make it cling to the track than anyone she knew.

Shouts from the house rose above the music, so she eased the volume higher. In recent months her mother had become paranoid and afraid to interact with the public. Her gifted mother, who was once written about as a genius with a miracle memory, had devolved into someone who could not even care for herself.

The problem was that her phenomenal memory, once capable of almost perfect recall, now could not be turned off. Memories with sound and pictures flooded her mind out of control. She was overwhelmed and melted down under the onslaught. Sometimes it took hours to snap out of it. Lately it took days.

The sound of sirens lilted above the music as she placed a carburetor squarely on a shelf. Taylor cried as fear seeped into her thoughts—fear that her mom would require full time professional care. But her worst fear was that she might become just like her mom.

Taylor worked hard to hide her gift, which now seemed more like a curse. Eidetic memory apparently ran in the family. Though some people would give anything to remember everything, Taylor sometimes wished she could just forget. She turned the music higher and sobbed as she put the garage in perfect order.

At fourteen, she didn't have a driver's license, but often took race cars around the track. Tall and strong for her age, she had no trouble with the controls. After the ambulance left, with her father by her mother's side, Taylor turned down the music and pulled the cover off her personal stress reliever.

She still had some body work to do, but the drive train was complete. With money she had earned working around the race track, she bought a wrecked muscle car for nearly nothing. Weeks of work, and the car was almost like new. The engine was modified and better suited for the track than the street.

Needing to get away from the stress of the evening, she raised the garage door and rumbled into the night.

★★★

When she pulled back into the driveway, her dad sat in the garage waiting for her. Turning off the engine she pitched him the keys. She said, "I figure you will want these. I just had to get out and clear my head."

"How fast did you go?"

"Within the speed limit until I got to the straight away near the track. I ran it out a little, but I was just trying to get Mom off my mind. The wind and fresh air helped more than the speed."

"One day you are going to get caught without a license and it'll be expensive."

"I know. I have some money saved up."

As he pitched her back the keys, he said, "Any problems with the car?"

"A few rattles at road speed. I'll fix them with the body work. Are we going to keep talking cars, or can you tell me about Mom now?"

Chapter 2

Taylor considered not going to college and being a driver or mechanic but her dad would have no part of it. He appreciated her help and even her insight and expertise, but insisted she focus on her studies. He wanted her to spend more time dressing pretty and keeping an eye out for a young man with a future. He assured her she didn't want to grow up with grease under her nails and "busted up bones" from hitting the wall.

High school became almost as much of a passion as racing. She took every course that would prepare her for college. Most boys were too frivolous, with posturing and big talk. One senior guy, not knowing her back ground, made the mistake of bragging that he had the fastest car in town.

Playing along, she acted impressed and let him continue to boast. After he detailed all the modifications that had been done to his Chevelle, she said, "My old Dodge is pretty fast. Does your car have one of those floor shifter things?"

He said, "I'll bet you any amount of money my Chevelle is faster in the quarter mile than your Dodge."

Taylor had been driving an older Dodge family car to school that he assumed was her's. After classes she went home and pulled her Hemi Challenger out of the garage. Repainted flat black with gloss black highlights, it looked sinister. When they met later at the old road near the racetrack, Taylor pressed the stack of hundreds into the palm of a boy who had come along to witness the race. Turning to her opponent she said, "Give him your money to hold. Let's see what that Chevelle can do."

Taylor had watched him drive around town. The boy was a pretty good driver, and his car was fast. He was very upset that Taylor had let him believe that she would be driving the family car. He tried to back out on the race, but Taylor reminded him of his challenge.

Off the starting line they were close, but only until Taylor got traction and pulled ahead. Desperate not to get beaten by a girl, he overcorrected steering and almost hit Taylor's fender. Sensing the danger, Taylor veered away near the shoulder and kept the gas to the floor. In her rear view mirror, she saw his car spin out. Headlight beams zig-zagged across the highway as he tried to regain control. Seeing she had won the race and his car was okay, she crossed the finish line, turned around and returned to where he paced by his car. She collected the money and checked his car over.

Taylor said, "Your car looks cool with the rear end jacked up, but it's affected your stability. Bring it by the house some time and I'll help you get it back safe again. Are you okay to drive home? You look a little shaken."

"Shaken? We could have been killed. I went completely sideways. I almost hit you."

"You need to get out in an open road or abandoned parking lot and learn to handle your car. Spin it around and see how it feels. That's the only way you will know how to deal with it when it happens. I can get you on the track sometime and let you practice." Holding out her hand to shake she said, "Friends?"

After that evening, everyone knew not to challenge Taylor. Her few run-ins with the law were always respectful. She made sure to keep her exhaust quiet unless she was about to race. One or two speeding tickets and she learned to do most of her racing on the track.

By the time she went to college, she drove a Corvette. Boys tripped over themselves to see her car. They soon forgot the car when they got to know the driver. She had a way of making everyone feel better.

Chapter 3

During her sophomore year at The University of the Carolinas, Taylor met a well-dressed young man in Anatomy and Physiology class. When it came time to select a lab partner, she turned to him and said, "Want to help me gut this frog?"

"Odd, I was just about to ask you the same question. Hello, I'm Rex Gulliver."

"Any relation to the Gulliver in *Gulliver's Travels?*"

"Yes, as a matter of fact, I am an explorer and adventurer. The world is on my bucket list and I intend to check it all off one day. What kind of name is Taylor? Got a last name to go with that?"

"Nope, that is my last name. It's all I've ever answered to, and I like it. The name helps me get more things done. People assume it's a man when they hear the name, and they're usually more willing to work for a man."

Rex asked, "What kind of work do you do?"

Taylor said, "Build race cars and engines."

"Maybe as I explore the world you can drive me around."

"Maybe after I patent some ideas and get rich, you can drive me around."

They liked each other's quick wit, and though they were often poking fun at one another, they were never mean. They complimented each other's skills. Rex was a great reader, knew a lot about everything, and was a visionary. Taylor learned any subject almost instantly, and was extremely organized and efficient. Rex soon gave up competing with her intellectually.

While she was still in college, some of the factory crews were at a race one night and she quizzed them about some of the inner workings of the standard three-speed automatic transmissions. She had an idea for an improvement that would make the transmission lighter, stronger, and simpler. Rather than share her idea, she asked for three new transmissions to use in a race car to try some modifications.

After a few months and a few hundred dollars in machining, her design was complete and the patent applications were in the system—patents pending.

She invited the factory men back to the track and sat her transmission on the scales. When she sat the stock transmission on the scales, it was fifteen pounds heavier.

One factory man said, "Anyone can take parts out of a transmission and make it lighter."

She pulled over a box of parts and said, "Like this?"

"Yes. Exactly right. A transmission won't work without these parts."

"I made a few modifications. This car has a transmission like the one I modified on the scales. Hop in, let's see if it works."

They got in and buckled up. She handed each one a crash helmet and said, "Sorry, track rules."

To make sure they didn't think she had removed reverse she stomped on the gas burning rubber backwards, turned the wheel, pulled it into drive and burned rubber for another hundred feet.

"So far, what do you guys think? Do all the parts seem to be working?"

The car shifted easily through all the gears. She downshifted in the turns and opened it up on the straight away. On the second turn around the track, she let the car get close to the wall. Coming out of the turn she drifted the rear end until it scraped the wall with a shower of sparks. Easily pulling out of the slide she dipped low in the turn and coasted toward the infield. Using the gears to slow into the pit area, she coasted to a stop and turned off the engine. "I've already put a thousand miles on this transmission on this track and on the road. You think anyone at your company would be interested in the technology?"

A factory man said, "I'm still not convinced you've made the changes in this transmission. We've had engineers constantly working to improve this system and make it lighter. Every pound counts. How'd you do it?"

"I have the detailed drawings, patents pending, documented witnesses and test data with pictures. I've been told some auto makers try to get ideas from people, make a slight modification, and patent their own version. I don't want that to happen. Get me a letter of intent and a non-disclosure agreement signed and we can talk more. It turns out that this change can also be done to your competitor's transmissions. So whoever gets this first can license it to others."

She said, "Here's my number. You know how to get in touch with me. I've already recorded our planned meeting with my attorney and I'll see him just after you are gone. You can't get information from anyone here at the track. They know nothing about what is inside. Once we sign the papers, I'll send this transmission back with you to test." She pulled the cover off another transmission. It was polished to a shine. All access points to the inside were welded closed and stamped. It would be impossible to access the inside without breaking the welds.

"If you X-Ray it, you won't see much. I look forward to seeing you soon."

When they left, Rex came over and clapped a well-deserved applause. "I believe you are about to be a very rich lady. Let me take you to dinner."

"Help me lock up. I feel like celebrating. We make a pretty good team. Your patent lawyer gave me a good deal. Your personal lawyer waived his fee. You paid for the machining and parts. Are you sure all you want is dinner?"

"My father gave me quite a bit of money with only a few conditions. Use it for good; help others help themselves; help those in need; encourage those you help, to help others when they can. He said if I did those four things and did them well, I would never run out of money."

"Does it work?"

"Ask me in a few years. You are one of my first dozen investments. I have a few in Europe, Mexico, Africa, and here in the U.S."

Taylor said, "Tell me about you, rich kid. Top student—budding philanthropist. What more is there inside that wild-haired yellow-eyed exterior?"

"Wild hair? I just tried to comb it a little while ago."

"I have known girls with red shaggy hair like yours. You might as well give up. It will always do just what it wants—and I think it's cute. You try to look all dignified like a rich kid should, but your hair gives you away. You're just a wild child at heart."

At the pizza shop they talked until the manager blinked the lights. Rex said, "Guess that's our cue. That was some fancy driving on the track. Remind me not to ride with you if you're in a hurry. See you after class tomorrow."

The next day they talked for a while and agreed to meet to study at Taylor's apartment. When he arrived she said, "Good news. The papers are signed and they want to meet and talk money. Can we get your lawyer to sit in?"

"Sure. I can tell you what they will do. They will offer you about ten percent of what they think its worth. You should counter with twenty times their offer. Eventually settle on ten times their original offer. The main thing you want is royalties on every transmission made whether it's with them or someone they license to. Don't be greedy, you can still be wealthy at fifty cents a transmission."

"So you're not just a rich kid, you're a smart rich kid."

"I have been around my father who is a savvy dealer. He's fair but tough. He grew up in the depression and earned every penny he has. I try to be a good steward of what he has entrusted to me."

She asked, "Where are you going during spring break?"

"Maybe to Egypt. I'm trying to get approval to enter a recently unearthed tomb. I may have to make a sizeable donation to the museum to get a look. I love this stuff—adventure and the hope of a new discovery. What are your plans? Designing new parts?"

"No. I haven't made plans. If I get this deal finished up, I'm free to go anywhere. I can gas up the Corvette and take a road trip."

Rex blurted out, "Come with me"—and was immediately embarrassed. They hadn't even been out on a date and he was asking her to go to Egypt with him.

"Yes." Taylor said.

"Yes you will go? I didn't expect to ask you and I didn't expect you to say yes."

"I want to see what it's like to be an adventurer. If you are having second thoughts, that's okay. I was thinking while you were describing the tombs and the museums that it would be fun—very different, but fun."

Rex said, "Let's do it. I mean let's go. Do you have a passport?"

"Yes. It's up to date. I've only been to Mexico and Canada."

"This is likely a silly question but, do you like to shop?"

She walked over to a mirror, took in a deep breath, looked at her profile, and said, "Still a woman, so yes, I like to shop."

"Then pack light. You can buy things you like and need along the way. Then it's easier to carry stuff back."

"That's very practical. Where'd you learn that, from the last girl you took to Egypt?"

"No. I learned it from my dad, who learned it from my mom."

Taylor gave him a big hug at the door. "Thanks for everything. If you get cold feet about the trip, let me know and I'll understand."

"Not a chance. This will be the best adventure ever." He kissed her quickly on the lips and was gone before she could say more.

Chapter 4

Rex heard Taylor's Corvette a few blocks away. She slid to a stop exactly on time to drive them to the airport. She had packed light and still there was barely room for his bags.

Later, settled in first class, they enjoyed breakfast as they watched the sunrise over the Atlantic.

Taylor said, "I didn't expect to be having breakfast with you watching the sun come up."

Rex was at a loss for words. As he stumbled for an appropriate reply, Taylor continued. "Where is our first stop after we land? I thought we were flying to Cairo, Egypt but the ticket connects through London and on to Tangier, Morocco."

"We have a one day layover in Tangier where I want to check out a story about a small Buddhist monastery with a spring of floating gold."

"Are we expected?"

"Of course. I've been researching the story and managed to get through by letter a few months back. They've agreed to speak with me. I'm hopeful I can learn enough to determine if the rumors are fabrication or have some factual basis. Gold is so dense; it's highly unlikely anything could float."

"Will we have to dress in orange robes and go barefoot over hot coals?"

"If we do, I believe I'll pass on the opportunity."

"After coming all this way I'd like to watch you do it. I'm just along for the ride."

Hours later, after a plane change in London, they caught an airport taxi to the monastery just outside Tangier.

As soon as the cab pulled away they turned to find themselves staring at the chest of an orange giant. Out of nowhere this massive man stood, toe to toe, staring down. Scrambling backwards, Rex took a moment to get enough composure to speak.

"Rex and Taylor here to see…" but the giant interrupted.

He spoke to them in a deep sing-song language.

Though he didn't understand a word the man spoke, Rex said, "We are here to speak with a man called Tulku."

Without another word, he turned and led them into a simple stone hut near the back of the compound. He gestured for them to be seated, but was gone when they turned around.

"How does he do that?" said Taylor.

Rex said, "For a man his size, he sure can move quickly."

They sat quietly whispering to each other and watching the only doorway into the tiny hut.

Taylor said, "We have company."

They turned around to see a small man standing just behind them. Again their natural reaction was to stand and take a step away.

The small monk they assumed was Tulku, gestured for them to sit on the floor in the center of the room. He joined them a few feet away.

Taylor had been taking notes the whole trip. She discretely scratched a few notes on her notebook.

The monk began to speak in a strange language and continued with gestures and expressions as if they understood. Taylor wrote notes as fast as she could. Rex looked completely confused and tried twice interrupted to let him know they didn't speak the language.

Taylor's note taking was a life-long habit. She made perfect notes without looking, even in the dark. It was like her hand automatically worked on a separate wavelength. Rex had once observed her writing another's conversation even while she was speaking.

Taylor looked at her notes and flipped back a page. She looked at the monk and, using the page as reference, began to speak in a staggered version of the monk's language.

She flipped back and forth between multiple pages and soon got the cadence.

A broad smile came over the monk's face.

Rex said, "Whatever you said was either good or you may have a new boyfriend. How'd you do that?"

Rex was interrupted by the monk in perfect English. "Taylor, you have an amazing talent for organization and language. Were you familiar with the Pali language before you entered the temple?

"No. I've read of it, and had one general course about the derivation of language. My focus has been physics, statistics, and business management."

Tulku said, "Today you are the student. Keep your mind open always. When it's time, open the mind of another like you."

"What do you mean, 'like you'?" she asked.

"Taylor, everyone is unique and has special characteristics that make them so. You, however, are a grape twice as sweet as all others in the harvest. You are a star that shines when others are dark. You are a spring of water that does not run dry."

"I just came along with Rex; he's the one seeking to learn about history, tombs, and artifacts. I hardly even know what this place is about."

Tulku continued. "Rex is extraordinary, but in a different way. He is a giver of gifts. He can never know some of the things you will know. His is not so much to know, as to help others know. Some think of all people the same. In many ways they are, but in many they cannot, and should not be. Taylor, you appear fit enough for the journey. Maybe you are ready to reach into the water."

"Is Rex going to reach into the water?"

"No, Rex's journey is not your journey."

They walked outside the temple and along a well-worn path following a small stream. It ended in a solid rock face with a narrow curved slot from the stream up about four feet. The slot was not large enough to crawl in. It was barely a foot wide at the widest place.

The monk said, "You must go inside and bring back a tiny bit of gold." He handed her a small flashlight.

Taylor said, "You may not have noticed but that crack isn't big enough to crawl into."

"Maybe you aren't trying to solve the problem. Maybe you are blocked by fear. You studied science. Think not of the obstacle but of the solution. Only bring back one bit of gold."

With that he motioned for Rex to follow him. Rex went to Taylor, "What do you want to do? Do you want to leave?"

"No. Go with him. I think I have a plan."

When Rex turned to walk with the monk, Taylor turned her attention to the problem. She hadn't considered entering the slot in an unconventional way. She stood sideways and bent at the knees, like sitting in a car. The slot in the rock was roughly the shape of her profile. Inching sideways she fit herself uncomfortably into the slot. Her face touched the stone unless she faced to the side. There was no more than a hand's width of clearance anywhere. She slid to her side. As she went deeper in the slot it became easier because she could push with one hand and pull with the other like sliding across a park bench. The slot became tighter and began to bind against her almost everywhere at once. Pushing harder against the friction she inched forward. Fear crept into the tiny space. She thought, *"This can't happen to me, not here, not like Mom."* Flashes of memories and sounds assaulted her brain. Taylor stopped pushing and took a calming breath. She tried to clear her mind but remembered her mother's struggle those last weeks at home. Memories of the broken window and the fading ambulance siren cascaded through her mind. Then she thought of better times. *"We went everywhere together Mom. You knew everything. You told the most descriptive stories of places you had never been in the world. Everyone wanted to be near you to be a part of your genius. Dad and I were so proud of you. We should never have let the government do all those tests on you. I don't think you were ever quite the same."*

Concentrating on the complete darkness and regular breathing, the images faded and she calmed. A few more deep breaths and Taylor saw only black—blissful black. Clicking the tiny flashlight back on, she thought. *"What purpose would it serve for me to get stuck in this rock? If there's a purpose, I must be able to continue."* More easily now, she inched further along. In the darkness the little flashlight beam illuminated the slot for only another ten feet. When she approached the edge, a little room appeared with a pool of water from which the tiny stream flowed.

Taylor was so relieved. No light came from where she had just passed. The crevice had curved, blocking any light. She said, "Hello. Is anyone out there? I made it to a pool." No answer.

Crouching by the pool she shined the light around looking for gold. It was a little pool with gravel sloping down from where she stood as far as her little light shone.

Remembering what the monk said, she tentatively reached into the cool water. She picked some pebbles from the bottom and examined them. They looked like normal creek gravel. She reached in the clear water again and noticed some movement beyond her hand. Jerking her hand back, she watched as the ripples cleared, and she saw nothing unusual. Again, she slowly slid her hand into the water, watching the depths for movement. Something appeared again—shadowy figures moving just outside the beam of the light. As she reached deeper, the forms came into view. Translucent spheres rose and fell slowly in the distance like the fluid in a lava lamp. Each seemed to have a tiny eye staring back at her.

She switched off the flashlight and could see nothing. She hoped there was some light from the water or the tunnel, but it was total darkness. When she turned the flashlight back on, the motion was nearer the edge. Without realizing it, she had moved ankle deep in the water. Sliding her hand along the bottom, while shining the light at the moving objects, she was able to coax one figure closer. The tiny eye was a reflection of a smooth gold sphere in the center of the orb. Reaching slowly with an open hand, she slipped beneath the mass. She felt nothing as her hand moved right through the translucent layer and came to rest against the surface of the tiny gold sphere. She resisted the urge to jerk away as a tingling sensation passed into her hand at the touch. "I am counting that off to my imagination," she thought.

It was only the size of a pea. Bringing her hand closer to her face, she was surprised to see the bead was perfectly round with no holes or seams. It felt much too light for solid gold.

Taylor put the gold bead in her pocket and began the journey sliding back through the notch, pushing with her hands, and being careful not to bump her head as she maneuvered through the squeeze. To her surprise, the passage never got tight against her on the way out. *"How could that be?"*

When she emerged it was dark. She thought she had only been gone for a few minutes but, with it dark, it must have been an hour. Using the flashlight she followed the stream back to the temple where she found Rex with the monk. Rex jumped up and hugged her. "What were you doing all this time? You were gone two hours."

The monk waited patiently as she walked to him and presented the tiny gold bead. "Well done. Please keep it with your silence and think about what you saw and experienced. It's yours for your lifetime to reflect. You may speak of it with Rex. We have been discussing your journey while you experienced it. He can be trusted with the secret too."

Tulku removed a gold pendant from his neck and hung the leather strap around Taylor's. It was a strangely curved broach that resembled the profile of the opening in the stone.

The monk recited something in the strange language and left the room.

As they walked Rex said, "That was not what I expected. I went there to try to research the rumors of a magical spring that "bubbles forth gold." What did you find?"

She produced the feather light orb. It already had a few dents in the surface. "This bead must be incredibly thin. It almost floats. Can you explain what happened back there?"

Rex said. "Only that you are incredible and exceptional and now have the respect of that order of monks. They will help you and serve you the remainder of your life, if you ever need them."

"Why? I didn't do anything special."

"I think you did. I think they realized you are very special and they are glad you are one of the good guys. Apparently, some people who come here are not so good and things don't end as well."

"How'd you get in the crevice anyway?"

She fingered the necklace at her chest. "I just had to sit down and think about it."

Chapter 5

When they left the door to the Monastery, the cab driver from earlier was waiting at the entrance.

Taylor started to look back but she knew the tall monk would be gone. She didn't know how they did it, but she knew enough about special abilities not to question it.

At the airport they retrieved their luggage from the lockers and checked in for the flight to Cairo. Taylor felt the pendant on her chest and it felt warm. It was solid gold and heavy. She examined the shape and the tiny slot with a thin blade like feature near the bottom. She could think of no use except maybe to sharpen a pencil point. On a whim, she plucked a hair from her head and held it over the slot. A gentle movement down and the hair fell in half from the slightest touch.

"Sharp?" asked Rex.

"No wonder the tiny blade is tucked in the slot where you can't touch it. It's a razor."

***

The tires chirped as they touched down in Cairo. While waiting for their bags, Rex called to confirm that his contribution to the explorers had been made. A taxi drove them to what was rated a five star hotel. In Rex's opinion, it would be three stars in the U.S.

Rex knew excavations like this tomb were notorious for underworld characters, thieves and corrupt local officials. It would not surprise him to find that his contribution went to pay bribes or government officials. The next morning Rex bought them some more appropriate clothing and they went to the site to meet the foreman. He quickly took them aside and told them to come back in the evening when the workers were gone.

Rex and Taylor went to a local antique dealer and talked with the owner. They bought a few trinkets and asked the owner if he had a personal collection. Suspicious of Rex's intentions he avoided the question. Later Taylor pointed to a back room and said, "What's in there?"

"It's off limits."

Rex said. "I am told in your personal collection you have memorabilia from early explorers. May we see?"

Calling an assistant to watch the front of the store, he led them through the curtains.

"As you can see I collect discarded items that others think worthless at the time."

A scarred pith helmet hung in a dusty glass case. It was classic style for explorers in the early nineteen hundreds. Many of the pyramids and tombs were being explored by scientists from Europe and the United States. Below the hat was a tiny label. "George Andrew Reisner, Circa 1910." Rex knew of him as one of the great pyramid explorers.

"How can you possibly know the pith helmet is authentic?" asked Rex.

"I was there as a boy. When he left, he gave it to me with his thanks for helping at the site. I never saw him again."

Rex offered him a fair price for the explorer's helmet. He did not sell until Rex offered twice his original offer. Then he reluctantly gave up the famous explorer's helmet. With tears in his eyes he handed over the piece.

When they left the store, Taylor said, "I will bet you ten dollars tomorrow he will have another helmet just like that one hanging over the plaque."

"Well I'll never know. As far as I'm concerned, this is the real deal. I won't be going back to look."

That evening they met at the tomb. It turned out the foreman was sneaking Rex in and that is why he waited until dark. They followed him in and through the narrow stone lined passage. Deeper in the vault the air got cooler and the smell was stagnant.

Rex asked about the air quality. "Have you ventilated the tomb since the discovery?"

"No. There was no money to spend until you came along. It isn't much further."

Taylor said, "Is it safe to be down here?"

"Perfectly safe", the foreman answered, "We have only lost one worker. We think he already had malaria before he entered the tomb. Two others left not because they were sick, but because they were afraid of curses. There were some inscriptions that warned of plagues on the families of those who enter."

"Aren't you afraid for your family?"

"No. I am all alone. I have no family to kill."

Taylor wondered how much of the talk was for effect. She didn't like the feeling she was getting from him.

They stopped at the doorway. Rex took pictures of the glyphs near the door. The entry was low and just wide enough for a sarcophagus. Taylor offered to wait outside. Rex took her by the hand and led her inside. The ceiling barely cleared their heads. Around the room lay artifacts intended to comfort the entombed in the afterlife. Rex took picture after picture.

The foreman said, "Please touch nothing. It must be as we left it earlier today."

"What's in the casket?" asked Taylor.

"No one has looked inside yet. There is much paperwork with the authorities."

Something didn't feel right to Taylor. She had a good sense of a person's character. This guy was setting off all kinds of warning signals.

She said, "Rex, I don't feel well. We better go. I'm sure they don't want vomit in the tomb."

Rex said, "Just a few more pictures."

Taylor walked up to him, looked him in the eye and said, "We go now."

Rex shrugged at the foreman and said, "We really don't want her to be sick in the tomb."

Just then there was a rustling from outside the low doorway. Two men came in with guns.

The tallest one said, "Looks like we have some grave robbers here. You two came along at just the right time. We needed somebody just like you to be found with some loot, while we make off with the real good stuff. You can even help carry it out."

Stiffening and standing as tall as he could in the low room Rex said, "And why would I help you carry anything?"

The taller one said, "Because you are strong, and she'll be tied up and left here to die if you don't."

He grabbed Taylor's hair and held the gun against her side. Rex said, "Don't hurt her. I'll do what you want."

The gunman walked Taylor over to the corner and sat her on a low box. He tied her feet and hands with a cord and gagged her. To humiliate her more, he bent down to kiss her on the head. She drew back as if repulsed and head butted him right on the nose. He went down bleeding and came up ready for revenge. His partner grabbed his gun hand and said, "No more. If we have time later you can deal with her. For now stop the bleeding and let's get this stuff out of here."

Rex had tried to escape during the excitement but found the foreman also had a gun and was in on the robbery.

Rex and the three men wrestled the sarcophagus from the stand. They removed the top to verify there was in fact a mummy inside. It was surrounded by gold objects and a few small ceramic vessels. Satisfied with their haul, they replaced the lid and dragged it through the doorway.

Outside the door they belted a small set of wheels to the sarcophagus and pulled it through the corridor. Taylor knew they would be a while getting it up the steps. She had memorized the corridor as they entered. Her near photographic memory would serve her well now. Every step, nook, and corridor was catalogued in her mind. She thought of her tortured mom and hoped she could avoid her mom's fate.

It got darker in the room as the men got further away. She thought, *"They plan to leave us dead in the tomb and blame us as part of the theft."* In the last bit of light that flickered in from the corridor she saw a reflection on her chest. The pendant the monk had given her caught the light and winked back at her face. The sharpened edge in the inside of the crook was about the size of the sturdy cords that bound her hands and feet.

She bent forward in the darkness and felt the necklace touch her bindings. After several attempts, it hung on one of the cords. Pulling back against the leather thong with her neck she cut through the cord. Wriggling her hands, she loosened the bindings, and used the pendant to cut the cords on her feet.

Free from the bindings she needed a plan and a weapon. The darkness didn't bother her because she knew the way out. Removing the lid from her stone seat, she rummaged around inside. She settled on a metal object shaped like a baseball bat. Hoisting it onto her shoulder, Taylor felt less vulnerable knowing she had a weapon.

Out the door and down the corridor she made it easily to the top of the stairs in total darkness. Hearing them returning she ducked into a small nook beside the top of the stairs ready to attack.

Lights danced on the floor and ceiling as they approached. A plan came together in the seconds before footsteps crunched on the sandy stone before her. Taylor thought, *"Rex will be forced in front where he can't escape. The three thieves probably won't even have their guns drawn. I'll wait till the first person is clear."*

As soon as the first set of feet passed she swung the heavy metal bat and hit two solid shins. As they bent and fell she came back and connected with another. *"Who's next she wondered,"* as hands touched her from behind. Stepping to one side, she rammed the bat backwards with all her strength and felt a crunch as she connected with someone's sternum. Like a berserker in Norse tales, she lunged at anything that moved. Light glinted on a gun and the bat crushed hard against the wrist. The foreman reached for a secreted gun in an ankle holster as Rex caught sight of him in the beam of a fallen flashlight. Rex kicked his hand away and removed the gun. Three men writhed moaning on the floor as Rex gathered up the remaining weapons.

Suddenly Taylor thought, *"Please don't start again. I can't lose control again."* The flashbacks started. Random memories from anywhere and everywhere, all at once, flooded her mind. Taylor was momentarily in a daze. The scenes, smells, and sounds of a thousand events flooded her consciousness.

Rex came to her and wrapped her in a tight hug. "It's okay. You had to do what you did. You were great."

She calmed and the visions went away. Regaining her composure, they hurried up the sloped ramp and through the iron gate. Locking it, they ran past the truck where the robbers had stashed the sarcophagus.

Standing in the darkness near the car, Taylor said, "Let's get out of here. I don't think we need to be caught up in this. We would probably end up in jail even though we stopped the robbers." She pitched the bat into their gear bag in the dark trunk. On their way to the airport, they stopped at the hotel only long enough to get their luggage. Just before the plane left, they called the police and reported the attempted robbery.

Sleeping while snuggled on the plane, they arrived in France within a few hours. Reasoning that the captives would try to blame the attempted theft on them, they went straight to a hotel room and checked in under an assumed name.

After resting, Taylor unpacked her bags. She opened the duffle and found the bat she had used to fight the men. As she removed it Rex let out a low whistle. The bat was a solid gold scepter. The big end was the shape of a small cage. Looking more closely, Taylor could see the rounded shape was really the form of a huge scarab beetle wrapped around glimmering rubies. The shell of the beetle was a grid-work of heavy gold lacings with rubies filling the gaps. Gold jointed legs, and pincers wrapped around the biggest ruby. The beetle blended into the twisted ornate gold handle.

"You really know how to choose a weapon." He took a rag and polished it up, removing some dried blood and hair in the process.

"I was fumbling in the dark for something to use. It felt like a bat so I took it. How are we going to get it back to them?"

Rex came to Taylor and held her tightly. "You were great back there. We escaped with our lives and accidentally one of the most fabulous relics I have ever seen, and you worry how we are going to get it back."

He wrapped it in a hotel towels and tucked it back in the duffle. "We better let things cool off a bit and see what the news reports say. The thieves may not know what was in the room. I think we better store it somewhere while we wait."

Chapter 6

"Tell me again what we are doing in France," Taylor asked.

"I would like to visit two clients while I'm on this side of the ocean. There's an archeological dig that's just getting started a few hours out of Paris. I'm a minor investor but if it shows promise, I might invest more. Let's go there and get out of the city. I don't feel good about staying here near an airport."

"So you take a girl halfway around the world to the most romantic city in on earth, and the first thing you want to do is go to an archeological dig."

He tried to recover and agree to stay a while but Taylor was ready to travel. She said, "I will take a quick shower and be ready to go in twenty minutes."

After hours cramped in the tiny rental Renault, they pulled into the little town. Dining at an outdoor café, they relaxed from the long car ride. Still suspicious of being followed, Taylor scanned the surroundings for any familiar faces. The dig site was about ten minutes out of town and they were not expected. Rex even wondered if they would find the site abandoned. His other concern was that Juliet, the archeologist, would still be mad. Months ago, he left her and went back to the states to finish school. She was a wild and unpredictable woman.

"Taylor, there's something I need to confess. The archeologist, Juliet, and I had a fling when I was here before. She was not happy when I left."

Taylor smiled, "So you are taking your new girlfriend, to meet your old girlfriend, that's still mad at you. Did she throw things when you left?"

"Yes, in fact she threw almost everything. Wine bottles, shoes, you get the picture."

"Should I get out the scepter and be ready to do battle?"

"That isn't a bad idea. Not to do battle, but to divert her attention."

"Can she be trusted? You know, not to turn us in, and get us put in a French or Egyptian prison."

"I think so. Her dad is a world renowned professor of archeology. She was raised right."

"I will keep the scepter handy and if I see you need an assist, I'll come to the rescue."

They drove to the site and there were two tents, one dusty truck, and a small travel trailer. The tents were set up at the base of a hillside between two streams. As they walked across the footbridge to the tents, Taylor whispered, "It's too quiet, this is like a horror movie where the murderer jumps out."

Rex led the way and Taylor followed with the towel-wrapped artifact over her shoulder. "Hello, its Rex." He announced after knocking on the trailer door.

From inside the trailer they heard a door slam. The front door opened to a raven haired lady with fire in her eyes. She spewed line after line of French that seemed to be more insults and cursing than anything else. Finally she cooled down and seemed to realize for the first time that Taylor was there. She suddenly turned her wrath toward Taylor and Rex intervened.

"You have every right to be angry with me but you have no right to speak like that to Taylor. Your father surely taught you better than that."

She quieted. "And I suppose your father taught you to bring a beautiful girlfriend to see the girlfriend you dumped."

"No, I learned that on my own. Juliet, this is Taylor. We are graduating together and yes, we are dating."

Juliet was beginning to get angry again so Taylor stepped forward and held out her hand. After a moment Juliet   relented and shook. Taylor felt the strength and calluses. She said, "Rex wants to talk business, but I want to talk girl talk. Let's sit down somewhere cool."

Seizing the opportunity to put Rex in his place, Juliet put her arm over Taylor's shoulder and led her toward the nearest tent, leaving

Rex standing at the doorway. Taylor motioned with the towel-wrapped scepter for him to follow.

Juliet pulled a bottle of wine from the cooler and three cups. She said, "What girl talk?"

Taylor rolled the towel across the table so that the scepter lay unwrapped just in front of Juliet.

With a straight face Taylor said, "I was wondering if you could help me identify the stone wrapped up by the gold bug?"

Juliet sank slowly onto the bench easing her wine glass to the table.

Taylor cracked a smile as she went on, "I got into a little scuffle and may have dented this thing up a bit but the stone still seems to be ok. I'm thinking about having it made into a necklace. This scepter is so out of style. You hardly ever see anyone carrying one of these around anymore."

Juliet looked up from the scepter and cracked up laughing. "You are either a very big joker or you are insane. May I examine this more closely?"

From a nearby box she brought out a magnifying glass and a notepad. As she read, she jotted notes and sketched. "Where did you get this?"

Rex said, "We haven't discussed this yet, but it might be best for you not to know until the dust settles a bit. Are you ok with that?"

"Rex, I don't think you are a thief, so I can only assume you are either keeping this out of the hands of thieves or holding it until the right time to reveal its discovery."

Taylor said, "We could have bought this from a museum."

"I don't think Rex has that much money. The ruby is worth millions."

Rex said, "We need a place to hide this for a while. We have to fly home soon and we can't take this. I want to get lawyers involved to get it to the proper authorities."

"Does anyone know you are here?"

"We stopped in town and had lunch. If someone tracks us to town, they will know I came to the site. I hate to drag you into this."

"I am going to leave now. You and Taylor make yourself at home as long as you like. When I get back from town tonight you won't be here. There are shovels there by the pit. If you use one, wipe all the fingerprints off before you leave. You know how I run a clean operation. We have exclusive dig rights on twenty or so acres. Feel free to take a walk. Is there anything else you need before I go? More wine maybe?"

Taylor came around the table and gave her a big hug. "How big is that ruby?"

"Maybe fifty carats."

Rex said, "I'll walk you to your car. I want to talk about the dig. What have you found?"

Chapter 7

Taylor said, "You said you had some business at the dig site with Juliet. Did you get it done?"

"Yes. She's progressing. The site is very slowly giving up a few secrets. She needs more laborers. There's an experienced older couple who work for her, but to do the screening and dirt hauling, she needs more help. I agreed to buy into the dig at a larger percentage. She can use the money to hire help and get more equipment. She loves it out here. I just hope authorities don't give her a hard time about us coming by."

"Do you really think they will follow us here?"

"They may follow our passports. They check them at every country we enter and leave. That's why we have to keep moving. We need to get back to school and finish the semester."

"Then why don't we go to the airport now?"

"I have one more stop at a mine north of Paris near the border with Belgium. Then we go home."

"What sort of mine?"

"Gem stones. It's a small operation. They needed an infusion of cash to keep it open and get some new equipment. I bought in for a share and it's been running better. I haven't taken any profits. I rolled it all back into the company. It's a small mine where people have scratched out a living for centuries. No records show when it began. They just started finding a few small stones in the gravel and built an operation around the area."

"Why are you going there now?"

"I am going to help them with some new equipment and pick up a present for someone."

"Another girlfriend?"

"So I guess now you think I have a girlfriend in every country?"

"Maybe just the ones you have visited. How many countries have you visited?"

Hours later they pulled into a little town and got a room. Rex paid cash and gave another fictitious name.

It was a tiny room and the smallest bath Taylor had ever seen. Taylor was determined to not become another statistic for Rex. She would be his girlfriend and his partner in evading the police, but she would not be a one night stand. When Rex came to bed, she feigned sleep, facing the wall. She thought, *"He's a smart guy. He'll get the hint."*

The next morning she woke to snapping suitcases. "Rise and shine. If we can get out to the mine soon we can catch an afternoon flight."

★★★

In Cairo the police were just realizing that, although the men they found in the crypt were known tomb robbers, they needed to interview the other two people involved.

Passport records showed two Americans, fitting the description of the couple involved, left on a night flight to Paris. The French police were in no hurry to get involved but eventually tracked them to a hotel downtown. The room hadn't been booked in the same name but the cab driver from the airport was sure it was the couple. He said the man's messy red hair was just as the officer described. They watched the room for a day and no one came in or out. Checking with the front desk the police learned that the room remained booked and prepaid for a week. The police decided to wait until they returned and grab them before they had an opportunity to fly back to the United States."

★★★

At the mine, Taylor met Pierre, a stereotypical Frenchman, complete with beret and scarf. Everyone greeted them warmly and Pierre led them quickly into the conference room. A freckled-face kid brought wine and pastries and waited nervously just inside the door. Pierre thanked her and asked her to leave them alone for a while. He explained, "The young lady is Fifi, a really great kid. Her mom did books for us for years. But now she has so many children, she has no time to work. Fifi worked along-side her mom even at an early age and is very capable of doing most of the bookkeeping at only twelve. She's like a sponge, learning everything she can. Earlier she asked if she could meet you and speak with you for a few moments. Anyone else I'd expect to ask you for money. Fifi must have something else in mind. I told her you were a very busy man."

Rex said, "I'll make time to speak with her."

Pierre got right to the point. "The police called and asked me to contact them if you showed up. I don't want to know what kind of trouble you are in, but if I can help, I will. You've kept us all alive and employed and we are making a little money now. We owe it all to you."

"Rex said, "Then I'll be quick. In Egypt, some outlaws tried to frame us as thieves and kill us. We escaped but I am sure they implicated us. We will go to Paris immediately to get a flight to America."

Pierre said, "That is what they will be expecting. Perhaps you should go home through another city or country. It's only two hours to Brussels."

"Ok. Business first. I'm prepared to buy additional stock in your company if you want to get more revenue and increase production. I'll buy up to ten percent more if you want to sell. I will also buy the sorting machine you requested. You can let me know by phone in a few days when I get home. Also, I need an uncut ruby. You can deduct it from my monthly allocation."

"You never take your monthly allocation. You are due much more than a ruby."

As he said this he walked toward a safe and moved packages around. He brought a bag to the table and spilled out a row of uncut rubies. Each had points of red blinking out beneath dark crust. Sorting through, he selected one of the larger ones. "Will this do?"

"Excellent. Now please ask Fifi to come in. I'm curious about what she has to say."

Moments later, after Fifi introduced herself, she asked Rex if it was alright to discuss financial matters in front of Taylor. Given the okay, she quickly made a proposal. "My mother owns a nearby plot of land that is no good for anything except growing brush." Pulling a handful of small rubies from her pocket, she said, "These rubies were found in a gravel creek bed on our property. My mother has worked for many years and I want to make life easier for her. No one knows about the stones except the three of us. Will you help my mother and me negotiate a fair sale of the property or the mineral rights to the mine?"

"I'll broker a deal, make sure you are treated fairly, and make sure there is no concern the stones came from this mine. I appreciate you coming forward with a proposal that could be good for both parties. Keep up the great work."

***

In the car Taylor proposed a plan. "When we reach Belgium, we call and make flight reservations to leave Paris in the evening. Then instead, we drive to Brussels, and fly to England."

They were greatly relieved when they made it through the border crossing with no problems. Taylor took a turn behind the wheel. The little Renault sputtered along and was nothing like Taylor's Corvette back in the states. At a gas station she raised the hood and made a few adjustments. Afterwards the little car zipped along as she maneuvered it through the mountain roads.

Rex said, "You got this thing running good but you better keep the speed down. We don't need any undue attention right now."

After reaching England, they booked a flight to Chicago. Only after arriving safely in the States did they book a final flight to Charlotte, North Carolina.

With the Corvette's top down and luggage stored, Taylor jumped over the door and slid behind the wheel. Rex buckled up when he saw the grin on her face.

Thousands of miles away the police tracked their movements all the way to Charlotte. No one followed. They were always a few hours too late to intercept them. The whole issue died down and the thieves were in jail. Apparently, no one knew that the scepter existed! That is, until they read the writing on the wall.

Chapter 8

Taylor's friends asked what she did over spring break. She said, "We flew to Tangier and hung out with monks, then flew to Egypt and explored a long-lost tomb. Then we went to Paris for a romantic evening and from there to southern France to dig for ancient artifacts. After a quick glass of wine, we went to a gem mine where we picked out a beautiful uncut ruby. We then raced through the hills to Brussels, and caught a quick flight to London—then Chicago and back here in time for dinner. What did y'all do?"

Everyone laughed at her outrageous story. She fanned the nine flight ticket stubs out like cards and said, "I didn't have an opportunity to spend much time shopping. It was a busy week."

They stared in disbelief at the ticket stubs.

Rex caught up with Taylor a few days later and thanked her for going with him. He apologized for putting her in danger and handed her a small box. She opened it to find a beautiful uncut ruby, polished with hundreds of tiny facets.

"I believe I have seen this before. It's beautiful."

"I wanted you to have something to remember this trip. I'll have it cut and set for you but I wanted you to see it first. I think they're almost as beautiful uncut."

"Rex, I know you have lots of money but this has to be worth a fortune. I appreciate the gift but it is too much."

"You made light of it but you fought three men and saved us both. A ruby doesn't begin to be enough to show my gratitude. We could both be dead if not for your quick thinking. By the way, how'd you get untied anyway?"

She pulled the necklace out from her blouse and showed him the cutting edge in the crook of the pendant. He said, "I believe the monk knew you would need this to get free. It may have saved my life and yours too."

"I think I'll accept your gift. Maybe, like the gift from the monk, it's meant to be. Thank you. It was a terrifying and wonderful trip. Do you have any more grand adventures planned?"

"Nothing major until summer after graduation. A struggling company in Mexico asked for my help. I sent them some funds but I want to see their operation again before I send more. It's a real challenge to know who deserves a boost and who is just trying to get free money."

"I believe two of the three places we visited were good people. I think you may have lost money on the tomb investment."

"I don't know. Someday we may have to go digging around in France and see if we can dig up a scepter."

"If you need another sidekick give me a call."

"What style do you want the ruby cut?"

"How about I keep it like this for a while? How many carats is it?"

"It's probably about fifteen carat weight. But who's counting?"

"Any ideas about this little gold bead I got from the monk? How can I keep from denting it more? I'd like to keep it with me but it's so fragile."

"Maybe it could be set into a ring where it's protected. I have a client in Alabama who can figure something out. He's a jeweler who just needed a little help to get his business back making money. He is retiring soon but he can do it. If you feel comfortable not having the bead for a while, I could send it to him with the ruby."

"Could you have him make a pendant of both the gold bead and the ruby? Could he make it structural like the ruby and the bead are in a sturdy gold cage? I can make a sketch. I want it strong because I'll probably wear it every day like this gold pendant."

She pulled him close and kissed him for a long time. "Thank you for a good time."

A man standing in the doorway watched the exchange and was especially interested in the ruby and the gold pendant she pulled from beneath her blouse. He had been a student in the past but had gotten into trouble and was unable to continue in school. Most of the students were unaware of his troubles. So, he often hung-out in the common areas and looked for his next mark. Deciding to steal the ruby first, he casually began to follow the rich kid.

During the remainder of the day he followed Rex as he went to classes. Waiting nearby he watched for the right time to snatch the little box Rex carried in his shirt pocket.

A crowd of students gathered in a hallway with Rex in the middle. The thief moved in the opposite direction and "accidentally" knocked the books from the hands of a girl six feet ahead of Rex. As the books tumbled to the floor, Rex and one other student bent quickly to help. In the tussle of people and feet all around, the thief slipped the box from Rex's pocket.

Taylor was just down the hall and saw the disturbance. Something did not feel right. She watched a student emerge from the group with no books. He looked familiar. She had seen him in the common area earlier in the day. Once again, like in the tomb, alarm bells sounded in her head. She watched as he smiled, slipping the small box into his pocket.

Taylor felt her pulse in her temple. A thousand images flooded her mind. She closed her eyes and calmed herself. The only times she had any trouble with her memory was on the few occasions when she had become furious or anxious about something. That guy stealing her ruby almost tipped her over the edge. Taking a calming breath helped to reestablish her composure.

The thief looked up to see her and couldn't believe his luck. He walked up to her and said, "If you have time between classes, could I buy you a milkshake in the cafeteria?"

Putting a pleasant look on her face, she said, "Why not?" and turned toward the cafeteria.

He reached around her as if to put his arm on her shoulder. Flashbacks of him watching her with the ruby and necklace tipped her off to his plan. In an instant, it became clear he was after her necklace. While his arm was raised she drove an elbow hard into his chest just below the ribs. He doubled over in pain, the wind gone from his lungs.

She grabbed his hair and reached in the pocket where she had seen the ruby disappear. Ruby in hand, she continued down the hall leading him, bent over, by the hair. The associate dean came out of the cafeteria as she approached the door.

The thief was just beginning to get his breath and realized the tables had turned. Taylor said, "Sir, is this the student who was expelled earlier this semester? He just stole this box with my ruby from Rex and was also trying to steal my necklace." Giving his hair a tug upward she had him face the Dean.

"Yes, that's the student, but we don't take matters into our own hands around here."

About that time Rex walked up and made his way through the crowd. "Taylor, what is going on?"

"Where is the ruby you had earlier?"

He reached for his shirt pocket and felt nothing. "It's gone! It must have fallen out when I helped pick up books in the hallway."

"It fell out alright. He diverted your attention, reached in and took it."

"They're lying, that's my ruby and she grabbed it from me," said the thief.

Taylor said, "Rex, do you happen to have the receipt from having the ruby polished earlier?"

He dug in his wallet, produced a receipt, and showed it to the dean.

"May I see the ring?" asked the dean.

Taylor passed the box to him and said, "It's not a ring. Just an uncut stone we got this week." The crowd moved in closer to see.

The dean said, "And where is this necklace he was about to steal?"

She removed the simple leather necklace from her blouse and held the pendant for him to see.

"And I suppose you got that this week too on spring break."

"Yes sir. A wise monk gave it to me."

"I see. Would you like me to call the police? I believe there's enough evidence to involve them at this point."

"No sir. I'd be satisfied if he was kept away from campus and a notation about being a thief added to his record."

Taylor realized she was still holding a handful of his hair so she released it. Humiliated, he kept looking at the ground.

The dean said, "Young man, if you will follow me, I'll escort you off campus for the last time. Students, I believe there are classes to attend."

Everyone gathered around Taylor to see the ruby and wanted to hear how she got it. She told a brief watered down version as she walked with Rex to a table. She said, "Are you sure you can get to a jeweler with this rock? I can drive it there myself if you would like."

Chapter 9

As graduation grew near, Taylor and Rex dated a few more times but became good friends rather than love interests. They complemented each other with their talents. Just after graduation Rex prepared to go to Mexico City. He supported a small charity and was prepared to make a larger donation. The non-profit helped build homes for people in poverty around the city. Taylor prepared to interview for a position as a purchasing manager in nearby Charlotte, North Carolina. As they talked about their plans, Taylor picked up a note from the placement office. She read aloud, "The position for which you applied has been filled, and there will be no need for you to interview. Thank you and good luck in your job search."

Rex said, "Go with me to Mexico. We can make it another adventure."

"How long will we be gone?"

"I planned a week, but we can stay as long as you like. It's not like you have to rush back."

Taylor said, "Don't rub it in that I just lost my first shot at a job."

"I wasn't rubbing it in. But since you are an official patent-holding inventor who sold a major patent license to the biggest transmission manufacturer in the world, it's not like you need a job."

"Thanks in large part to you and your lawyers."

"Well, will you go? We'll take care of business and then we can go anywhere we like. Want to crawl through some Mayan ruins?"

"No tomb robbers this time, ok? Will I be required to calm down any irate girlfriends on this trip?"

"It is guaranteed we won't see any old girlfriends on this trip. Juliet and you actually hit it off well in France after she cooled off."

"You mean after she saw the gold artifact."

"Touché."

"I'll make a flight reservation and pick you up at seven in the morning. Pack light and you might want to leave the ruby at home. Not the kind of thing you want to wear where we are going."

They arrived in Mexico City and had no trouble in customs. A man with a sign that read "Rex" met them outside the terminal and helped with their bags. He led them to a new four door pickup truck and put the luggage in the back. Most cars around them were at least ten years old, dented, and smoking. They rode in air conditioned comfort.

Taylor was glad to get out of the crowded airport. Her sense of the trustworthiness of those around her was warning her of danger. She figured it was just the crowd because when they left the airport, the feeling went away.

The office for the little company was like a thousand other storefronts in the suburbs of Mexico City. Inside the office the air conditioners kept the room cold. The ragged furniture had been replaced with new leather.

"It looks like business is good." Rex said to his host. "Would you mind if I have a look at your financial records?"

He and Taylor were presented with cold colas and a plate of tiny flautas. As Rex scanned the records, he soon found what he was looking for. The new truck and office renovations were paid for with funds designated for building homes in the slums. The total number of homes built in the last year was actually less than the year before.

Closing the books, Rex said, "I gave you money specifically for building more shelters in the slums. It looks like you have bought things for yourself and given yourself a raise with the money.

"No Mister Rex. We used the money from you to build the shelters. We used the other money from other donors to buy the truck and other things."

"Let's take a ride to the projects and see some of your work. When I was here before, you were just getting started. We should be able to see some real progress."

They went outside to the parking area and he led them to an old rusted truck.

Taylor asked, "Why are we taking this truck."

"The people don't need to see the new truck. When I drove it there they were angry and thought I didn't deserve a nice truck."

Taylor and Rex shared a knowing look.

The people were friendly and Taylor soon had a lap full of children. They played with her blonde hair and giggled. She understood some Spanish and soon could follow their chatter. In a sing song rhyme they chanted, "Rex has a girlfriend, Rex has a girlfriend."

Rex spoke passable Spanish and chatted with several people. They were not happy with the builder. They were glad to get help with their houses, but they didn't think he treated people equally. Rex expected this. He often was challenged as to why he gave to one group over another—a difficult question to answer.

When they were back at the office Rex said, "I'm disappointed that you misappropriated the funds. I'll make one last contribution and, after that, you are on your own." He left a check on the table and called a cab to take them to the hotel.

Taylor said, "That was a tough call. I think you did what was right."

"Soon you may be making that sort of decision. Like the monk, I can see you have a good heart. It'll be interesting to see how you deal with being wealthy."

She said, "So are you only dating me for my money?"

He pretended to ponder the idea for a moment then said, "No. It's nice to know that you have enough not to be dating me for my money. I just really like you. You are tough, beautiful, adventurous, and you can fix the car if it breaks down."

"Oh you do know how to flatter a girl as we arrive at the hotel. Do you think the room will be any bigger than the one in France?"

"Yes. I booked a nice room for tonight. Who knows what kind of accommodations we will have if we go exploring."

The next day they slept in and had breakfast delivered to the room. They made notes and put together a plan. A guide agreed to take them white water rafting on a river south of the city. The highest rated rapids were class four which was serious rafting. It would require an experienced guide to get them through right-side-up and should be very exciting. The brochure showed a map of the region, beautiful scenery, and lush jungles along one side. In the fine print it also warned of the dangers of class six rapids possible in rainy weather.

They were picked up by two men in a truck with a rubber raft in the back. The raft had patches in several places along the side.

It was an hour's drive to get the raft in the water. The guide went with them in the raft and the driver went to meet them in two hours at the take-out point. Rex checked to make sure they had a patch kit and pump, life jackets, an emergency medical kit, and snacks. They put most of their valuables in the dry bag and clipped it to the storage area of the big raft. The guide spent only a moment showing them how and where to paddle on his command, while he steered the boat. Taylor had a waterproof instamatic camera around her neck along with the gold pendant tucked tightly into her suit. Knowing they would stop on some gravel bars, they both wore comfortable sneakers. Taylor slathered on the sun screen and passed it to Rex. Rather than get the bag back out she tucked the bottle into her shorts pocket.

The raft bobbed easily in the fast moving water. As the guide steered the raft, they started planning their next adventure. They settled on a trip to the pyramids in the Yucatán Peninsula.

Soon they heard a roar from the river ahead. The sound increased and the guide shouted something to them with a broad grin.

Rex said, "This is where he earns his tip money."

The roar amplified and the river disappeared from view ahead of the boat. To the right loomed a dense jungle. Spray from the rapids blended with the fog rolling down from the mountains.

The guide sang out paddling commands in Spanish that meant nothing to Rex and Taylor. They both paddled furiously to try to keep the boat pointed down the river. They dipped into a sink and the boat bent double before popping out almost straight up into the air. All they could do was hang onto the ropes around the boat.

The water smoothed and the boat glided easily down the river. The guide was silent. Ahead of them, torrents of brown water tore across the smooth plane of the river. Heavy rain in the mountains flooded the river banks and trees and debris tumbled in the water ahead. The wall of brown water hit the side of the raft and doubled their speed. They kept the raft straight down the river but the guide looked worried. Rex asked him if they should pull to the side and walk to find some help. He said there was no help for many miles. The next road crossing was where the truck would be waiting.

Thunderous sounds came—twice as loud as before. Dirty spray rose from the rapids ahead. The guide motioned for them to paddle the boat toward the jungle side for smoother water. To their left Taylor watched water dip down and shoot up like a fountain between rocks under the water. She paddled harder to get further away. In front of them the water swirled. A massive funnel appeared out of nowhere. They paddled hard to miss it but the raft got sucked in. Round and round they went. They slid toward the bottom and then spun almost to the top. Dizzily they tried again and again to paddle up the spinning wall.

Taylor loved excitement but this was scary. Memories of every picture she had ever seen of boats capsized and people drowning flashed in her mind. Screams seemed so real. She realized they were her own. Rex wanted to comfort her, but all he could do was hold on. He caught her eye and screamed for her to snap out of it—to focus on him. "Watch for my signal and be ready to paddle for your life."

Occasionally rocks appeared in the funnel wall that could rip the boat open. When the back of the boat was high on the rim, Rex gave the signal and they paddled backwards with all their might. The boat tipped over the edge and back toward the major rapids. They paddled hard toward the smoother water of the jungle side. Without warning water erupted from beneath the raft. It lifted straight in the air and flipped over. Rex and Taylor held onto their paddles, but the inverted raft went down the river and out of reach. Swimming for the jungle, they went through one more set of rapids before grabbing limbs and pulling themselves out of the water. The last sight of the destroyed raft was a single paddle waving, raised above an inflated raft section as it disappeared into the brown spray.

Chapter 10

Rex sat on the bank staring at the river where the raft and guide were last seen. Taylor took off her life jacket, checked out their surroundings and said, "You wanted adventure. It looks like we got more than we bargained for. What are our options?"

"We can wait here until they send another raft down to pick us up."

She said, "With the river this high and clouds threatening more rain, they would be foolish to put a raft in the river. It'll soon be dark anyway. I'd say they won't be coming until tomorrow if at all."

He said, "Why would they not come back for us?"

"Your wallet and valuables are in the boat. I'm sure you had plenty cash in there. I didn't really trust this outfit."

"We could float in our life jackets down to the take-out point."

"I don't think we would survive. The map of the river shows ten more rapids before the bridge. Three are higher class rapids than we've paddled so far. There's also one more river that dumps more water in from the mountains where it's raining."

"You certainly paint a rosy picture," said Rex. "What do you suggest?"

"We can't go up river through the jungle because we can't cross the muddy river that ran out of the mountains. Same problem if we tried to walk downstream. We'd soon come to the next river. I think our only choice is to try to cross the mountain behind us and get to the road about five miles away."

"What makes you think there's a road on the other side of the mountain?"

"I looked at the map they showed us before we started to the river," she said.

"And you remember the road, and you happen to know just where we are."

"I remember most everything."

"Sure, like you have a photographic memory."

"No. It's actually called eidetic memory. And very few people know that about me."

"You're not kidding? I knew you were smart but I had no idea you had a photographic or, what did you call it, eidetic memory. Why didn't you tell me?"

Taylor said, "I learned, early on, that most people make a game of it or constantly test me. My preference is to quietly use it as I need it. Now I guess you're going to test me."

"Maybe it will help us get out of this mess," said Rex.

"Let's try to get to the road before dark. Maybe we can catch a ride into Mexico City." She looked into the jungle. The map hadn't indicated anything about the height or slope of the mountains. With the dense vegetation all around, there was no way to see the eight thousand foot mountain that loomed ahead. She used her boat paddle and scratched a map in the dirt. "Here are the three rivers, the mountains, and the highway. We are about right here," she said as she put an X in the dirt.

They decided they should go toward the river they had passed and follow it back into the mountains, rather than going over the mountain.

The life jackets were hot but kept some of the vegetation from scratching them so badly. The muddy tennis shoes were life savers. Taylor used her boat paddle to part the vegetation, clear spider webs from the path, and as a walking stick.

At first the trail was level, but soon became steep and rough. An animal trail led near the river, but it sometimes made long, looping bends as it snaked around pungent swamps. Only tiny streaks of sunlight managed to penetrate the canopy. Mysterious animal life moved around in the treetops far overhead. The out-of-banks river had slowed to a swift brown ribbon.

Final screams of distant animals filtered in from the jungle reminding Taylor of the cycle of life. Big animals ate the smaller animals. She wondered, *"Are we the biggest animals in the jungle?"*

Rex said, "Here is a short-cut across the swamp." A vine covered tree lay across a narrow section of the swamp and connected perfectly with the path beyond. The bark was worn smooth where animals had crossed. Without hesitation, Rex started across the makeshift bridge half submerged in the swamp. Taylor followed using the boat paddle for balance.

Halfway across, Rex stumbled but stepped onto a small log for balance. Taylor froze in place as she realized the log he was stepping onto was a snake as big around as her leg. Rex screamed as he felt the soft body of the snake and realized his error. As he fell into the water and scrambled to get back on the log, the snake quickly wrapped around him squeezing him to the log. To his horror, he felt himself being dragged deeper in the water.

At first Taylor fought the images in her head. They came faster and faster bombarding her with overwhelming numbers of scenes of snakes and danger and so many subjects she could not comprehend.

She thought, *"Snakes are crawling in my head, screaming and hissing. Putrid smells are gagging me."* Rex's screams brought her out of overload and back to reality. As she focused on what was playing out before her, she saw the snake's massive head rise from the water and move toward her at eye level. It turned suddenly from her to its screaming captive, directing its open jaws on Rex.

Without a conscious thought or plan, Taylor swung the paddle like a Louisville Slugger. The edge of the paddle connected solidly at the base of the big snake's skull with a sickening crack. The paddle split into two pieces as the snake slumped into the water.

Taylor, off balance from the swing, splashed into the swamp. With the snake's grip loosened, Rex scrambled free and crawled onto the fallen tree. Taylor struggled to get back on the log. Behind her Rex saw the head of the monster raise up and move toward Taylor. Grabbing the splintered boat paddle from the water, he stabbed the pointed end just past Taylors face and into the striking maw of the Anaconda. Taylor pulled herself up as she looked over her shoulder to see water roiling around the thrashing beast.

"Run. Let's get out of here," said Taylor as she sprinted across the log.

For a long time as they put distance between them and the serpent, neither spoke. Taylor went into the underbrush and Rex thought he heard her throwing up. When she returned, he held her close and said, "Thanks for saving me back there. I thought my exploring days were over."

Taylor said, "I guess since I whacked that snake, you had to take a stab at returning the favor."

"I'm glad we both lived to joke about it. That was as intense as it gets."

"I froze up for a second back there. I was afraid I couldn't get out of my own head and help you. I don't know what was worse, what went on in my head or the anaconda. I can't get the smells and taste out of my mouth."

Rex said, "I am really sorry for putting you in that dangerous situation. We both could have been killed."

"I don't think you really understand the danger I was in. I wasn't afraid to die. I was afraid I would live and go insane from the way my brain reacted to the danger."

Rex said, "It must be really strange to remember everything?"

"Researchers think everyone records everything in memory, but never access much of it again. After a time the brain loses the ability or the inclination to remember. For those who can intentionally recall everything, imagine if we lost the ability to filter unwanted thoughts. It's like drinking from a fire hose. The images are overwhelming, terrifying. That's what happened to my mother and what's beginning to happen to me."

Rex said, "I'm sorry it was so traumatic for you, but I'm glad you came to my rescue, again. We came out much better than the snake. I will be surprised if he survives the way he thrashed about with the paddle through his neck."

Taylor thought, "*Something very bad happened in my head back there, just like my mother.*" But she said, "I wonder if that anaconda just lay there every day, waiting for something to cross the log before he struck? Like a swamp version of *'The Three Billy Goats Gruff'*."

•••

After a few hours the terrain worsened and they stopped to rest. A small stream from the rock ledge trickled clear water. Taylor knelt and tasted the water. Cupping her hands she drank her fill.

Rex asked, "How do you know the water is not contaminated?"

"I don't, but it looks better than that brown stuff in the river."

"I agree. Save some for me," said Rex.

Standing and stretching, Taylor said, "We aren't even half way. I remember that big sweeping river bend on the map. We better start looking for some food and a place to sleep."

"What's that on your leg?"

Looking down she saw a black worm like thing on the back of her leg. Rex looked closer and said, "It is a leech, and there's another one."

"Get them off me, where'd they come from?"

"They got on you either in the river or the streams we crossed. We better check each other. They can attach without you feeling them because they have an anesthetic in their bite. Holding one up he said, "This one is full of blood."

He found two more small ones on her and she found three on him. As they got back on the trail he said, "You know leeches are edible."

"Go ahead, you can have mine too."

They decided to try to find some fruit instead, but the canopy was so high they found nothing for a while. At the next stream crossing they were glad they still had their life jackets. They swam across and checked again for leeches. Resting near the water and looking up in the clearing above the stream, Taylor saw some fruit in a treetop. She didn't know what it was, but she walked around to the trees and searched about underneath. Lots of seed pods lay around with only tiny bits of fruit still attached. Something had stripped away the fruit from the seeds.

Rex came to see what she found. "Why don't we pull the vines that go up in that tree and see if we can shake something loose?"

They tugged on vines, but most coiled so tightly to the tree they didn't shake the branches. Finally Taylor found one that went into the fruit bearing limbs. She shook a few pieces loose. Soon it rained fruit.

They gathered several that seemed ripe and went back to the log where they had rested earlier. Taylor said, "Any idea what these are and if they're poisonous."

"They are longer than apples and, from looking at the seeds on the ground; they have a pit like a peach. I have no idea what they are, but I don't see any dead animals lying around. I'll try it first—like Adam."

"Well how is it?" she asked.

"Taste like chicken."

That got him a punch in the shoulder.

"Actually it tastes a little like a mango, but not nearly as sweet. I think I'll eat a little and take more with us. I'll be the guinea pig and see if it makes me sick before you try some."

"That is very nice of you, my own royal taster. Seriously, thank you. Let's pack some of these and get going. Start looking for a camp site."

Rex made his tee shirt into a bag and filled it with fruit. They came to another tree with a smaller berry growing. Looking around they saw where animals had eaten and deposited the seeds. Something about these berries didn't seem right to Taylor. She said, "I don't know why, but these berries seem like they aren't good to eat. Let's move on."

"I am okay with that. So far I feel alright after eating the fruit in the bag."

Taylor said, "Not feeling like you need to exchange the shorts for a fig leaf?"

It was getting darker and they found an overhanging rock ledge to shelter from the weather if it stormed. The dirt was soft and bare as if other animals had kept the vegetation worn away. For this night the shelter was theirs. They stacked the fruit from his shirt near the rock and leveled out the dirt as best they could with rocks and sticks. Taylor said, "So far we are good on water and this fruit is not bad." Squirming to one side she retrieved a bottle of sunscreen from her back pocket and held it up.

"Hang on to it. When we end up out of the jungle in this heat we'll need it."

"Did you get away with anything?" she asked.

"Just what you see."

"Almost the same for me. I have my necklace and my lanyard and pendant." She reached into a tiny pocket in her swim suit bottoms and pulled out a wet folded square of money. She unfolded it to reveal a five, a twenty, and a one hundred dollar bill. "I learned a long time ago to keep a little money tucked away just in case. It won't do much good in the jungle but it may be helpful later."

With no way to build a fire they snuggled close in the dirt and went to sleep.

In the night there was a scratching nearby and Rex felt something against him. Thinking it was Taylor he rolled toward the noise.

A loud screech blared in his face. Taylor awoke screaming, though she didn't know why. They had no light but they found each other in the dark by sound and feel. They could hear animals making all sorts of noises around their feet and bumping against them.

Then, as suddenly as they had come, they were gone. The jungle was silent. Gradually the buzz of insects resumed. The chirping of frogs increased. Soon the jungle was back to full volume. They squatted back down and felt for the rock they had to their back. Once in position they laid back down.

"I believe a bunch of monkeys stole the fruit," said Taylor.

At morning light they assessed the damage. The fruit was all gone. Rex had unloaded the fruit so he at least hadn't lost his shirt. They were hungry and mad at the monkeys for stealing their breakfast.

Bugs swarmed. Rex said, "I wonder if sunscreen might work as a bug repellent? Let me try some and see if it helps. Flies are getting on the bloody leech bites."

Chapter 11

Taylor swatted flies gathered on the black splotches where her leeches had been. Red welts radiated from infected bites. Rex said nothing but was worried about the red streaks.

Slogging up-river, they finally found more of the fruit like they had eaten the day before. These were ripe and tasted better so they ate their fill and packed a few along for lunch.

They came to another small spring and were able to get some fresh water. Near midday they came to another creek and swam across in order to stay near the river. Taylor said, "It looks like all these streams are full of leeches," as she pulled three more from Rex's leg.

Taylor, drenched with sweat, drank water at every opportunity. Rex felt her forehead. "You are burning up with fever. How much further do you think it is to the road? We need to get you some medical help."

"It is quite a bit further. I'm getting pretty weak but I can make it."

Rex said, "I'm sure you can and I'll help you." Pulling her close to his side, he carried some of her weight as they continued along the riverbank.

The river was still flowing swiftly but was not whitewater. They targeted an open area far downstream to allow for the current. With the lifejackets, they were not concerned about drowning. They were only concerned with making it to the other bank before being carried past where they could climb out. Halfway across Taylor ran out of strength. Rex grabbed her vest and swam hard, barely reaching the low bank before it transitioned to jungle. He hauled her into a field of brush where they rested. Moments later, Taylor set them on the course that should take them directly to the roadway. Rex helped her cross the rough terrain.

He checked Taylor's forehead and she was still feverish. He cooled her down with a water-soaked tee shirt and tied it around her head.

They applied more sunscreen to keep the bugs away, as their bites were getting more infected.

In the distance they saw a break in the terrain, and helped each other along until they finally came to a little dirt road. They started down the road toward Mexico City—no traffic in sight.

Along the side of the road there were some small berry bushes. Rex gathered some berries that looked edible and tried a few. They were tasty, like blackberries, so he gathered some and brought them to Taylor.

After resting for a few minutes they continued. Both could barely move. The sun was out in full force and they were out of sunscreen.

Looking back, Taylor noticed dust rising above the road. Waving down the truck, Rex asked the farmer for a ride to the hospital. Two farm workers helped them into the back of the truck.

After about thirty minutes of bouncing on the rutted road, the truck braked to a stop in front of a small building. The sign read "El Centro Medico." Rex said, "Taylor, we made it, it's a hospital."

The workers helped get them to the lobby. Taylor offered to pay them for the ride, but they declined. Refusing to take no for an answer, she pressed some money into the driver's hand and thanked them. The clinic workers came out to the lobby and explained that this was not a regular clinic. Rather, it was a special cancer treatment facility. After seeing their condition, they agreed to get them well enough to go to a regular hospital.

They were treated and fed for a few days and allowed to recover.

Rex talked to the doctors and learned about the clinic. It was started five years before as a mission where people in advanced stages of cancer could have experimental treatments outside the United States. The doctors explained that Mexican laws were more lenient and allowed them to try things that were illegal in the United States.

Their success rate was not very high but the people who came there were terminal. Saving people was their goal, and every year the results were better. Rex thought it was a good cause so he talked to the doctors about funding. This was one of two clinics that were already open in the country. They had dreams of opening more, but funds were very limited.

Rex told the doctor that he invested in good causes like this and would like to get more involved by making a contribution.

Taylor's fever broke day two in the clinic. The swelling and redness in the infected leech bites looked much better. Though the doctors wanted her to rest, she walked the halls and exercised almost constantly. Normally strong and self-sufficient, she was embarrassed that Rex had to almost carry her part of the way out of the jungle.

By the third day the doctors agreed they were well enough to go to Mexico City. The nurses gave them additional clothing to wear. The van that brought supplies to the clinic every few days, took them to Mexico City. They were dropped off at the hotel where they still had a room booked. The hotel concierge connected Rex with his lawyers in United States, who transferred money to a local bank. They found that their hotel room had been tossed and, although nothing was missing, someone had searched it thoroughly.

They spent the next few days in the hotel recuperating. By the end of the week they were back to normal. Taylor continued working out, getting back in great condition.

Taylor said, "Let's pay a visit to the rafting company and find out if they ever even came to look for us." They took a cab to the address where the rafting company was supposed to be and found nothing but an empty storefront.

According to the people next door, the two men who ran the operation took their boat and personal things from their office and left about a week earlier. The only explanation given was that business was slow and their boat was damaged.

Taylor said, "I guess we know what happened to the money that you had in the boat. They probably decided that would make a good retirement fund."

"There was about a thousand dollars in my wallet, so I guess that was enough money for them to close up shop and move somewhere else."

"You lost your wallet and license but at least our passports were still in the room. Here we are, in a foreign country, and you have no money to show a girl a good time."

"I had plenty money sent to the bank. We are okay for cash."

"I heard you talking with the doctors about investing in those clinics. That seems like a really good idea. They treated us well. What kind of success rate do they have with cancer treatments?"

"It's really not a very good success rate but it's because their patients are terminal. When they come to the clinic, doctors have already given up on them. As a last resort they try experimental treatment and only about eight percent survive. He believes if patients could have access to earlier treatment, many more could be saved."

"So how are you going to help?"

"They want to build additional clinics along the United States' border so it's not as difficult for people to get all the way to Mexico City for treatment. I've agreed to help them fund a clinic in one of the border towns."

"That sounds like it might be a better investment than your guys who were building homes and driving a fancy truck."

"Yes, I was pretty disappointed in that group. When I first came down they seemed to be very promising. We'll see if they start doing a better job. If they do I will continue to fund them."

The doctor from the cancer clinic met Rex in the lobby. They exchanged contact information for lawyers and worked out financial details. The doctor requested the clinic to be located in one of the border towns with a scenic mountain view. He believed seeing the beauty of nature outside patient's rooms would help their recovery.

Chapter 12

Once Taylor and Rex recuperated they debated whether to strike out on more adventures or to go back to North Carolina. They agreed that one more excursion was in order. Since they were in Mexico City they decided to catch a flight south to visit the pyramids in the Yucatán.

They drove to a small pyramid and ruins with a nearby cenote. Rex had to explain the history of what looked like a sink hole with water a hundred feet down. Taylor declined swimming and said, "After all the leeches in the jungle, I think I will stick with bottled water and sandy beaches. No more jungle swims for me."

Rex said, "I made arrangements to accompany an archeologist to a newly discovered site."

"Translated, that means you paid him lots of money for a sneak peek into a tomb."

"No. I did pay some money but it went to a museum which happens to sponsor him. This site is new and they have only found a short corridor and a big pile of rocks. No tombs or sarcophagi have been reported in these ruins."

•••

The jeep bounced over rutted roads that occasionally had sections of stone pavers. Deep into the wilderness of towering trees and tangled vines, Taylor asked the archaeologist, "What's the largest predator out here in the jungle?"

"Except for the hunters with their rifles, the jaguar would be most feared. They have a terrifying scream that has been known to make some men die right in their tracks."

Taylor said, "Great, back in the jungle."

Rex leaned up behind Taylor. From his pocket he pulled out a ceramic figurine in the shape of a Jaguar head. The novelty from a village shop replicated a jaguar's scream when a person blew into the chamber. Not willing to pass up the opportunity to startle Taylor, he blew hard into the opening. The hoarse screech almost caused Taylor to jump from the jeep and the driver to veer off the road. Instinctively Taylor swung an elbow back and connected with Rex's chest. The offending jaguar call flew from his hands and disappeared into the jungle alongside the jeep.

"You want to go back and get that thing?"

Rubbing his chest, Rex said, "No. I don't think it is good for my health."

The jeep lumbered into a small opening in the trees. Tents were set up around a large pile of rocks in the jungle. In three directions there were patches of stone from the ancient roadways. The rock-pile where the roads converged seemed significant to the researchers.

While digging through the rubble archaeologists came across an arched entranceway that led underneath the surface of the jungle and into a stone encased tomblike area.

No one had yet explored this corridor in detail. The archaeologist invited Taylor and Rex to accompany him inside. Adorned with lights and hard hats, Rex and Taylor stood outside near the arch.

Taylor said, "This is so much like Egypt. Are you sure these aren't grave robbers waiting to set us up and kill us?"

"How do you feel about them?"

"Actually, I feel good. The lead guy seems like a really good man."

"Then off we go."

Inside the archeologist pointed out different features of the passageway carved into the stone. It wasn't a natural formation like a cave. It appeared that the passage was created by rocks stacked tapering toward the inside, with layers of large stones across the top to create a tunnel. It continued for several meters back into the ground and then just terminated in stone, like a tunnel to nowhere.

After studying the construction of the tunnel and the stones where it terminated, Taylor said, "I wonder if, rather than this being the end of a passage, perhaps it is the beginning. Maybe it opens up vertically to the jungle floor."

They scratched around inside the area. One of the last flat stones across the passageway before it terminated seemed like it was a little different than the others. Taylor stepped off the distance from the termination of the passageway to the point they entered the archway underground. She paced on the jungle floor the same distance they had walked underground and stabbed a stick in the ground. "This is where you should dig to access that last stone."

Workers dug for about an hour while Rex, Taylor, and the archaeologist walked around the other parts of the site. When they heard shouting they ran back to the dig site. The workers had come to the stone they were looking for and cleared the dirt from around it. Hand holds cut into the top of the stone allowed easy access to lift the stone.

The archaeologist patted Taylor on the back and said, "You have quite an eye for this."

Rex said, "She's very perceptive, very smart."

In the opposite direction of where the stone was discovered, a little bit higher up, a large mound of rock rose from the jungle floor. Taylor speculated to the archeologist, there might be another passage at a higher level near that area. Seeing the possible connection, he said he'd let her know what they found.

Rex said, "Let's assume, as Taylor suggested, this is the beginning of the passage. Where do you think the other end leads?"

They walked back to where they had first entered the passageway. After looking closely at the site, they found it was not an entrance the archeologist had found; but rather a ceiling that had collapsed into the passageway. Digging in the opposite direction and moving stones out of the way, they found that the passage continued.

They took a break and had some refreshments at the jeep while the workers cleared away the stones to access the passage. After about fifteen minutes, Rex led the way as they trekked into the passage, snaking deeper into the jungle floor.

Taylor said, "I don't like this very much. The ceiling could fall in and collapse the passage. How do we know it is secure going forward? We could touch the wrong thing and be trapped."

The archaeologist said, "Are you afraid of being trapped in a tomb?"

Taylor said, "Been there, done that."

"You've been trapped in a tomb?" asked the Archeologist.

"It's a long story we won't get into right now, but it all worked out for the best."

He said, "Well maybe we should call it a day, come back, and follow up on this later."

Rex said, "This is the closest I've ever come to an original discovery. Taylor, you may want to go and wait outside but I want to keep exploring."

"No, I'll stay with you for a while. If it seems dicey, we should all leave."

The passage finally split into two smaller tunnels. The archaeologist said, "Taylor, right or left, what do you think?"

Veering left, they continued through the passage. It narrowed and was blocked by rubble where the ceiling had collapsed. They had no choice but to turn around and go back to follow the other fork. Finally it began to expand to a larger passage, which opened up into a room with columns that supported the ceiling. The room was a network of columns about six feet apart with barely room to get between them. The columns were made in sections of circular stone that had been stacked on one another to make a ceiling about seven feet high. Large stones spanned between columns. Some were collapsed. They were able to work their way around the piles of rubble as if in a maze. Carvings appeared in the walls and columns. On one side they saw an area recessed into the wall with stones carved around the opening. Inside, small jade statues, stone vessels, and three gold figurines sat huddled together.

Taylor raised a small instamatic camera and took pictures as flashlight beams darted side to side. The archaeologists suggested maybe this was a good time to leave, citing the compromised ceiling. He said they would put together an appropriate team and investigate it properly.

Taylor said, "Now that you've documented it with pictures I think you would be wise to take at least one object with you to verify the find just in case something happens."

Rex said, "You never know when something will happen. Someone else may decide to come back first. You may not be able to come back in for some reason."

"It sounds again like you speak from experience."

"Yes, Rex and I have experienced something very similar."

"Then get your camera ready and document me collecting these artifacts."

Taylor flashed a picture of the archaeologist lifting a tiny gold figurine and then the other artifacts in the nook.

As he turned, his shoulder bumped one of the columns. Dirt fell from the ceiling and dust clouded the room.

Rex grabbed his hand and led the way out of the room as rocks peppered down.

As they entered the larger passage toward the exit, rocks tumbled and dust boiled behind them.

Taylor, Rex, and the archaeologist exited into daylight, to rumbling beneath their feet as the last of the passageway collapsed belching dust from the opening.

As the workers gathered to make sure everyone was out and safe, the archaeologist pulled a small gold figurine from his pack. A cheer rose from the workers.

Taylor stepped to one side and walked along the jungle floor in the direction they had taken underground. Surprisingly there was little evidence on the jungle floor of the recent collapse beneath. She stepped it off carefully, making angle turns now and then.

"What is she doing?" The archaeologist asked Rex.

"I told you she's perceptive. She remembers every step and turn. My guess is she's about to show us where the room is underneath the jungle."

She walked across the jungle floor and, as before, stabbed a walking stick into the dirt.

Rex and the archaeologist joined her near the stick. Taylor said, "The stick is very near the spot where the artifacts were taken. We should move away in case the jungle floor falls into the room. See the cracks in the dirt?"

Taylor and Rex certainly made a new friend. The archaeologist was ecstatic. He had been digging out there for weeks and, within a few hours of Taylor's and Rex's arrival, they discovered beautiful artifacts. Rex agreed to stay in touch with him to see how the dig was going.

Back at a hotel Taylor relaxed for a while and Rex began working on a proposal for the cancer clinic. Taylor looked over his shoulder and offered to help. He named things that needed to be done in order to get started. She picked up a notepad and took notes. It was the first time Rex truly realized how organized she was. He said, "Let's try something. I'll tell you all the things I can think of to get this operation going and you come back to me with a plan to get it done and let's work together on this."

She said, "Are you putting me to the test?"

"Not really so much of a test as possibly an interview."

"Interview for what? Is this one of the qualifications to be your girlfriend?"

"Right now I'm thinking more of a partnership. I have a lot of money to spend and a lot of good things that I want to do. I often find myself getting sidetracked with having fun and adventures and I'm not organized enough to accomplish everything. If I could couple your organizational skills with my money and business acumen, I believe we could get some phenomenal things done."

Taylor said, "So this sounds like it's more of an audition than an interview. Just how much money do you have to give away?"

"It's not as much a matter of giving it away, as it is giving it to the right people who can put it to good use. In many cases I get a large payback on what I give away, like at the mine. I could always collect money greater than what I've invested, but I choose to let it roll back into the mine and let the business flourish."

"With a cancer clinic, think of the people that could be helped if we can make this work. One problem is that most procedures aren't covered by insurance. Most people don't have enough money to afford this kind of treatment even if they can get out of the country. Often the money is their last savings. They sell their homes or do whatever they can to try to live a bit longer. Maybe there's something I can do to help develop a clinic that operates in such a way that it doesn't cost so much for people to use it."

"Rex, you're a good guy. Because you're such a good guy, I'm going to do your little audition. Tell me more. Tell me all the things. Tell me your heart's desire."

He told her how much money he had to spend and the things he'd like to do with it. Together they listed all the steps they could think of to get the clinic started. She called the concierge and had more paper sent up for her list.

By evening, when they were done, Rex looked through the stacks and stacks of paper. "Wouldn't it be amazing if we could just do all this stuff? Think of all the good we could do."

She said, "Have I not mentioned how good I am at spending money? Just as easily as I can make all these lists, I can get it done. You should've seen the way that I organized things at the race track. I helped the owners spend a couple million dollars upgrading the race track and we got it done in record time."

Rex said, "I don't think you'll have to go on any more job interviews. My goal is to spend all this money investing in people and organizations. Between the interest coming back from the principal and return on some of the investments there should be a never-ending supply of money to give away. The principal will remain intact."

"How much does this job pay?"

Chapter 13

Rex said, "How about this: I'll pay you what you were planning to get where you applied for the job. In addition I'll pay all your work related and travel expenses, and on the jobs that I plan to earn money, you get a bonus based on how quickly and efficiently you get the job done."

"That sounds fair. When do I start?"

"You already have. The first project is the clinic in Tijuana, Mexico. Find some land near the mountains—maybe about five acres. It needs to be remote with highway access, water, and electricity."

"Is there a separate budget for land, the clinic, and equipment?"

"One budget—five million total. Do some research and let me know when it can be built and ready to occupy. Here is a list of what they have at the clinic we visited and the costs three years ago."

Taylor said, "Then I guess our next stop is Tijuana, Mexico. No point going back to North Carolina."

"You really are hitting the ground running."

"You haven't seen anything yet. We will have this clinic up and running in no time."

After landing in Tijuana, Taylor spent most of her time on the telephone. She was learning Spanish quickly but hired an English speaking real estate agent. Rex hired a bodyguard to go along with her when they had to be separated so that she would be safe traveling in the country.

The real estate agent showed her a ranch located in beautiful mountain foothills. The price was good and it met all of Rex's criteria except it was three hundred acres.

Taylor liked the ranch house and the quarters that were attached. She thought it would make a good medical wing for the clinic. The plan was not to build a surgical center. It was more for non-surgical type treatments so they didn't need multiple operating rooms.

The asking price was reasonable but Taylor told the realtor to offer two-thirds of their asking price. They went out to look at one other property but it was run-down and didn't meet Taylor's needs. Back at the hotel, Rex and Taylor had dinner. Later that evening the phone rang. The realtor said, "They accepted your offer. We close in three weeks.

Taylor turned to Rex and said, "You just bought yourself a ranch."

"What do you mean I just bought myself a ranch? I thought we were looking for a hospital."

"What I found is going to speed up the process and I think you'll love it. I found a ranch with three hundred acres, a big house, and an out building that can be turned into a wing of the clinic. The house could be the main portion and the wing can be where all the residents stay. It has electricity, water and is easily accessible to the highway."

"Did you get a good deal on it?"

"Yes I paid two-thirds of their asking price. They can close in three weeks."

"Have you checked to see if it's zoned for commercial use?"

"Yes, that was one of the stipulations."

"I guess I shouldn't be questioning your capabilities."

"That's ok. It'll take you a while to find out how efficient and proficient I am. It doesn't hurt my feelings that you double check."

The next day Taylor and Rex rode out to the property and he was very impressed. He said, "This will be a great place. Just look at the beautiful backdrop of the mountains. Why are they selling it?"

"Well it's a sad coincidence. The husband of the lady who lives here just died of cancer a few weeks ago. She can't run the place by herself. They're down to just a few cattle so she was ready to sell."

"Did you tell her what the land was going to be used for?"

"No, she was willing to negotiate the price based on me offering cash and a quick closing."

The lady who answered the door remembered Taylor and asked them to come in. After the small talk, Rex asked her what her plans were after she sold the ranch. She said, I plan to move in closer to town to a facility where my husband spent his last few months. They took very good care of my him."

Rex said, "Taylor didn't tell you yesterday what our plans are for this place, but you might be interested to know we're going to build a cancer treatment clinic. We want people, who are in the late stages of cancer, to have access to alternative treatments, especially if they can't afford the high cost of some of the other facilities."

After a few moments she said, "I've had so many friends who died of cancer and either didn't have the money or the opportunity to go somewhere to get help."

Rex said, "I think the ranch, with the beautiful scenery, will help keep up the morale of patients and speed their recovery. Some great doctors will come here. You are welcome any time to visit or for a medical need. Just let us know."

She said, "There are some great trails up in the mountains. Hopefully when some of the patients recover, they will be able to go to the mountain and enjoy the view looking out across the valley."

Head down, she reluctantly asked a question. "Would it be too much to ask you to consider hiring my son if he's willing to work here? He's a physician's assistant at a hospital in Tijuana. Administrators are not willing to try new and different medicines. It has been his dream to work in a place like you describe. It would mean a lot to me if you would talk to him."

Taylor spoke up. "We would be glad to interview him. Just give me his name and number. I'm sure he'll be a great asset to our team. I know we're set to close in three weeks, but I'd like to get contractors out here as quickly as possible to look at the land and make plans to convert this beautiful home."

Taylor worked long hours, lined up workers, and hired a local general contractor. The two realtors got together and were able to fast-track the closing. As soon as the check cleared, contractors began work.

Within weeks it began to take shape. The interior of the home was remodeled and brought up to standards that made it easy to clean and maintain. The house became the office, recreation area, kitchen and dining room. The quarters near the house were extended and connected to the main house, making twenty hospital rooms. Each one had a view out the back looking over the mountain side.

Three weeks into the build, the doctor from the Mexico City clinic showed up. He couldn't believe how much progress had been made in such a short amount of time.

Rex bought and paid for the facility. The doctors leased the clinic. Rates were set low and the percentage the doctors kept was tied to their success rate.

Taylor met with administrators at the hospital in Tijuana and nearby San Diego, California. She asked for help getting the clinic off to a good start. They agreed to refer patients and to help facilitate transportation across the border clinic-to-clinic.

Once the clinic was near completion, Taylor hired Miguel, a physician's assistant and nurse supervisor, who had also grown up on the ranch. He was an immediate asset to the team and well versed in cancer treatment. Taylor could tell he was compassionate to both patients and the nursing staff.

Chapter 14

Before the cancer center opened, all the staff was hired trained and ready as final construction was being completed. Taylor demanded the foreman explain why the construction workers didn't show up. He said, "The local gang decided it was time for you to pay a bribe for protection money. A gang member contacted my supervisor of construction and told them if they showed up for work they would be attacked morning and night. If you want to complete the project, you better pay them."

At first Taylor was furious to hear that her carefully planned Grand Opening was to be delayed. She talked to some people in the community and found who was in charge of the gang. Rex hired a local lawyer to determine the best course of action. He advised her that, in most cases, it was better to go ahead and pay the bribe just to keep the place open. He said, "Gangs cause all sorts of damage and are part of bigger syndicates. Bribes and crime are part of doing business in this part of the country."

Taking matters into her own hands, and acting against the lawyer's advice, she requested he arrange a telephone conversation with Scar, the gang leader.

Scar started the conversation with a lot of threats and big talk. After he finished his threats and demands, she asked, "Who is the closest person to you that has died from cancer?"

He didn't say anything for a few minutes and then he started the big talk again. She asked him again: "Who is the closest person to you who died from cancer?"

After a few minutes he said, "My mother died a few years ago."

Taylor said, "We can't guarantee that we can do any better, but this clinic is designed specifically to try to help cancer patients when their insurance or doctors have given up on them. It's modeled after one in Mexico City and it'll be using all the latest drugs and techniques to help people live. Would you have wanted a few more years with your mother?"

After a moment without a sound, Taylor continued. "We are trying to make this affordable so not just the rich can get treatment. We know insurance doesn't cover much of what we will do here. I realize you and your organization are powerful. I ask that you allow us to operate freely and give cancer patients a chance. We have nothing to offer except cancer care. People will only feel safe to come here if we have a peaceful relationship with the local people. If we cannot operate freely, the owners will just move to another region. They will lose their investment but that would be a one-time expense. Is anyone listening on the line with you or where they can hear you on speaker phone?"

"No."

"If I loan you something of great value, would you keep it for me as long as there's a peaceful and cooperative relationship? It's a personal item of jewelry that I had made. It is both sentimental and valuable. You can let others believe it's tribute or payment or whatever you want. Between you and me, it'll be a sign of mutual trust."

She was giving him an out—a way to save face. The pendant had both the ruby and the gold bead encased in a gold cage on a heavy chain. It was worth thousands of dollars.

He said, "I should not trust you and you should not trust me."

"I don't pretend what you do is right. I'm willing to make this concession as a token of friendship, to get the clinic open and help those in need of treatment."

Scar said, "I will meet you somewhere."

"Will I be safe?"

Without hesitation he said, "Yes. I'll see to it."

"And if the pendant isn't to your satisfaction to make our deal, will I be free to go with my jewelry?"

"Yes. I am anxious to meet a woman willing to risk her life to save people with cancer."

"Then you need to meet some of the doctors and nurses who go to work daily to save people with cancer. I can introduce you, and pray that you never need their services for yourself or your loved ones. The clinic isn't just for old people; they will treat children too. Shall I leave the jewelry somewhere for you to examine? There's a jewelry store nearby where I could leave it for you."

"Like I said, I want to meet the lady with the guts to make such a deal. Does this pendant belong to you or the company you work for?"

"It's mine. When we meet, I'll tell you the story of how I got it, and what it means to me."

Taylor had lunch with Rex and his lawyer and told them what she planned. They both advised against it. Rex said, "In the best-case scenario, you lose your pendant. In the worst case you are kidnapped or killed."

Taylor said, "I feel good about the deal. I believe he will honor the bargain and allow the clinic to run without harassment.

The attorney asked why she was willing to give up her own personal possessions for the clinic.

"I believe it'll make him a better person. He's not stealing or extorting it. And he knows that it isn't really his, just a symbol of our agreement. Rex knows I am a good judge of people. I sense he will treat us fairly."

Rex said, "And you trust this sense over the phone. What could go wrong?"

•••

She took the Jeep to meet him at a small Cantina on the outskirts of the city near the ranch. When she arrived there was a similar Jeep already parked near the door.

Walking inside she waited a few minutes to get accustomed to the dark and looked around the room. A man about her age with a deep scar across one cheek sat near the back in a corner. Except for the waitress, she was the only female in the bar.

She walked straight to his booth and asked if she could sit down.

Accepting his gesture to sit, she said, "I like your Jeep."

"Would you like a drink?"

"No, I'm driving. Thank you."

"She reached around her neck and lifted the necklace over her head, cradling the pendant, and handed it to him.

It was warm as he touched it and Taylor noticed a change in his expression. Looking up at her he appeared suspicious.

"May I tell you the story behind this? The ruby is quite large and quite valuable though I don't have an appraisal. It was a gift from some grateful people we helped in France. More importantly, the gold bead came from a very special spring in Algeria. It's in a monastery and guarded by monks. I was chosen to find my way into a chamber and bring back a floating piece of gold. The gold was only a token of the experience. The vote of confidence of the monks was the important thing. I am to learn and someday teach others. The day I received the ruby, a thief tried to steal it. I was able to convince him to give it back and later had the two pieces combined as you see them now."

"Why are you willing to do this?"

"Rex and our lawyer both asked me the same question. They said I was crazy. I believe the clinic is important. And I believe you keeping this for me is important. I don't know why. Maybe we will talk again someday and you will have a story to tell me."

"I expected you to tell me the loan was for one year and you wanted them back."

"No. it's more like loaning something to a museum. It may be of great value but the museum can benefit more than the owner."

He looked at the amulet closely. "You are willing to give this to me to help me save face with my men? It would certainly do that. I appreciate your offer. However, my men are my men, and they will do as I say. If I tell them to leave the clinic alone and even protect it, they will. I will let you keep your beautiful necklace and we will be a friend to the clinic. Someday we may need their services."

"I hope you or your family never need the clinic. But if you do, you need only to contact me or the clinic. I'll let the doctors know you are welcome."

Taylor continued, "Just a few weeks ago I was injured badly after a rafting accident and a trip through the jungle. The doctors at one of these clinics nursed Rex and me back to health. That's how we got involved."

"Maybe you should have a small general clinic for emergencies and children at this facility."

"Is this pendant starting to rub off on you, too?" She waved it teasingly in front of him like a hypnotist.

"Maybe not the pendant."

"I will talk to Rex and the doctors. At least in the beginning our beds will not be full. I think a small emergency clinic might be a good idea. I better go now. They will be worried about me. Is there a trail I could take on the way back to get a little dirt on the tires of this Jeep?"

He smiled and hung the necklace around her neck. As he did, he noticed the gold oddly shaped pendant hanging from the simple heavy leather string. "And what is this?"

"That has an even stranger story. It'll have to wait for another time. I guarantee you will love it."

"Then see if you can keep up. I will show you the trail."

After a dusty few minutes racing around cactuses and boulders, Taylor flew onto the highway and sped toward the hotel. Rex and the attorney were waiting in the lobby. "Where have you been? We have been worried sick. Are you okay? Why are you so dirty?"

She said, "After we talked and came to an agreement we went off-roading. He's a pretty good driver. If I had known the road better, I believe I could have taken him."

"So he agreed to your deal?"

"Not exactly. He's very smart. He figured out that I was letting him save face with his men and offering him a way out. In the end he agreed to let me keep the pendant. After I told him it's history and about our emergency treatment after the jungle, he requested that we designate a

room for emergency care and stock it with supplies to take care of locals
who couldn't get to the city for care."

"So we are a go for having the opening on time?"

"On schedule as promised and under budget. The clinic has beds for
twenty people and will have one fully equipped emergency room. It has
a staff and is ready for patients."

Rex pulled a note from his jacket pocket and handed it to Taylor. It
said, "*Son, I didn't put too much restriction on the funds you are to disperse.
I wanted to let you find your way. I've been keeping tabs on the account
and the work you are doing. You don't get an omelet without breaking a few
eggs. I believe now you are on track. Keep it up. That young lady you hired
complements you well. Take good care of that one. She's a gem.*

Rex Gulliver"

"Your dad I presume?"

"He gets a report every week. He contacted me last week and
questioned whether the numbers were correct concerning the speed
with which you built the clinic. I'll have to be careful that he doesn't try
to hire you away from me."

"So does that mean I get a raise?"

The lawyer said, "I believe my work here is done. I'll see you at the
grand opening."

The former ranch owner and her son Miguel were there to cut the
ribbon. Near the end of the ceremony an ambulance arrived quietly
with their first patient. A twelve year old girl from San Diego was
brought in on a gurney. She was bald but smiling at everyone. A rusty
pickup truck pulled up and a youth of about fourteen got out from the
driver's side and helped a very old man with a cane to the entrance.
Nurses quickly met them with a wheel chair and brought them inside.

In the crowd Taylor saw a familiar scarred face. He tipped his hat and
ducked back through the crowd.

Unconsciously, she touched the pendants beneath her blouse.

Chapter 15

Taylor and Rex returned to North Carolina and Rex continued to make calls and deals. Two weeks later Taylor dropped by to see Rex. "I have driven through the mountains for two weeks and I miss the excitement."

"You mean the exploring?"

"No. I miss the projects. With the clinic done, I have all this spare time and I really want to spend some more money."

"Maybe I have something that will be of interest. I found a wilderness camp in Colorado, in the foothills of the Rockies. They are struggling because of what appears to be mismanagement and possibly embezzlement. Consequently, they are short on money. The bad thing is that they started out with such a successful program. Five years in and everything is falling apart. I'm thinking of trying to get the camp back on its feet and giving these kids a chance."

"When can we leave?"

"I can't go for a week. How would you like to be a camp counselor for a week while I work on the deal?"

"I went to a camp once. It was rustic but not wilderness. How hard can it be?"

"Well, you are tough and in perfect condition. You might want to read up on survival skills before you go. Also read up on survival camps, what works and what doesn't."

"I better start driving."

"Leave your car at the airport. Fly to Denver and I'll have a car for you there. Take a day to get ready and study. For you, that should be plenty of time to become an expert."

With a mock salute, she said, "Yes sir," hopped over the door, and slid easily behind the wheel of her Vette.

•••

At baggage claim a lady held a sign that said Mr. Taylor, Camp Backbone-of-the-Devil.

Holding out her hand she said, "I'm Taylor," greeting the woman with a firm handshake.

"I'm sorry, I was expecting a man."

"I can see that."

"Actually I'm glad you are a woman."

"I am too."

"I mean, we have too few women at the camp. It's a tough life and most women aren't prepared."

"Well I've had one full day to get prepared so this should be fun."

"We sleep under the stars and don't have the amenities of home."

"Do you have toilet paper?"

"That is one thing we have but only in very limited supply."

"We can buy more," said Taylor.

"No, the idea is to have the bare minimum, if you will pardon the pun."

"I think we'll get along fine. Hi, I'm Taylor, and you are?"

"At the camp we go by nick-names only. They call me Brook, because I slipped in a brook and broke my leg a few years ago."

"Who were you before that?"

"Annie, because I shoot like Annie Oakley."

"Why not stick with Annie?"

"The men seem to like names for the women and girls that are funny to them. They get to choose."

The luggage rounded the carousel and Taylor grabbed both bags. "Lead the way Annie."

"I can see you are going to be a trouble maker," said Brook.

"I can be trouble, but mostly I fix things. First I figure what needs doing, and then I do it."

"I thought you were a counselor to work with the kids."

"I am, but I always try to leave things a little better than I found them."

In the parking lot they walked to an old but restored, jacked-up four wheel drive

pickup truck. Taylor said, "Is this yours?"

"No. I was told it was yours. They asked me to pick you up, in your truck."

"Well I was expecting a Corvette but this will have to do."

"This will do very well. A Corvette would not get halfway where we are going."

"Can we stop for some supplies?"

"We have most everything you need. Not much is allowed."

"I need a good sleeping bag and a small pillow. Also some bug spray and sun screen."

"Counselors are allowed a few more luxuries than campers. They have to earn everything."

Taylor said, "I earned the sleeping bag two months ago in a jungle in Mexico. I hope there are no leeches in the mountains." She showed Annie the scars on her legs.

"Who's in charge of the camp?"

"A man named Boss is in charge."

Taylor said, "Wonder how he got that name?"

"He makes all the rules and is very strict."

"How many campers do you have?"

"We have boys and girls. Usually we have fifteen of each. They're all here either to learn to behave better, to avoid detention, or to re-set their attitude. Sometimes kids get so far down a path they need a completely different environment to start over and find out what few things really matter."

Taylor said, "Like food, water, shelter, and people they can depend on."

"Exactly right."

After loading up on supplies, Annie said, "Take the next left and head straight for that white capped mountain. You won't need four-wheel drive for another ten miles."

•••

Taylor drove into camp and parked by some other vehicles. Annie said, "Pop the hood and give me the keys." She raised the hood and removed the distributor cap. "This helps cut down on kids leaving camp either by themselves or with counselors."

A few kids ranging from fourteen to eighteen came by and admired her truck. The crack of a whip brought everyone to attention. All eyes were on Boss.

Without a word, kids moved back to what they were doing before Taylor arrived. Boss moved in close to Taylor and growled in a whisper, "For now we will call you Blondie, till I come up with something better."

"My nick name is Taylor. I'll save you the trouble."

Seeming to decide whether to challenge her, he looked her over head to toe. "You do look like a Taylor. That will do for now."

"Brook, find this girl a place to sleep—supper in ten minutes."

Taylor brought her few things to the campsite. Her bags were left locked in the truck.

An open fire blazed, and to the side, on a glowing bed of embers, soup bubbled in an iron pot. Taylor was starved. Snacks on the plane were all she'd had since breakfast.

Boss ladled soup into bowls and the kids lined up respectfully to get their portion. Some got full bowls and others got half bowls. One defiant kid complained he only got half a bowl.

Boss said, "Do your share of the work and you will get your share of the food."

When it was Taylor's turn to get soup, Boss looked her over again as if how she looked decided how much food she got.

Taylor said, "Just give me half a bowl tonight. I haven't had a chance to do my share of the work yet."

Boss seemed okay with that idea and gave her a generous half bowl. As they sat around the fire eating, Brook said quietly, "You are pretty smart. Most counselors complain about everything and end up leaving in a few days."

More counselors showed up with the remainder of the kids. They appeared out of the night with no flashlights or torches. A large string of fish marked a successful day at the river.

Taylor asked Brook, "I didn't remember any river crossings along the way. Are we near a river?"

"No. There's one about six miles away—looks like it was worth the trip."

Boss said to everyone in general, "Finish your soup and let's get those fish cleaned and salted down."

Taylor tossed and turned on the hard ground. The sleeping bag was perfect but she was used to a soft bed and no amount of shifting seemed to make the dirt softer. She stared at the stars and let her mind go back to her research. She planned to have a soft sleeping arrangement the next day.

Before daylight, Taylor was just outside camp finishing her exercise routine when Boss cracked the whip at six a.m. He shouted, "Five minutes, gather around the fire for breakfast. Those with cooking duty, make sure everything is ready."

Taylor looked at her watch and figured she could make it to the top of a nearby rise and back right on time. Boss saw only movement in a dust trail in the rising sun.

At breakfast, kids eagerly spooned out scrambled eggs and fried fish. Boss announced the schedule for the day and said, "Enjoy the eggs.

Brook picked them up in town when she went to get Taylor at the airport. Unless you find some eggs out here in the wild, there won't be grub like this for a while."

Brook stood and introduced Taylor. "For those of you who came in late from fishing last night, Taylor is a new counselor. She'll be helping in general and will be coaching anyone who needs additional work on fitness. The daily work out here is demanding. She can help with exercises to help you endure it more easily."

Taylor stood and took a deep bow as if she had just finished a Broadway performance. Then she bowed further until her hands were on the ground. Pressing into a handstand she did five vertical push-ups bent at the waist and lowered seamlessly into a sitting position.

Everyone clapped except Boss who cracked his whip.

"That's enough grandstanding. Today we move camp to the far end of Devil's Backbone. Along the way we need water and food."

Boss introduced his right hand man to Taylor. "This is Viper. He'll assign you tasks throughout the day. Do whatever he says. Watch for kids straying from the group. There's always one or two who decide to strike out for home. That isn't an option."

Viper extended a hand to Taylor and did his best to crush her hand. She matched his grip and said, "I see your daddy told you to always greet someone with a firm handshake. You should take it easy on us girls. We are, after all, frail and soft."

Viper grunted and stalked off.

The group moved slowly so Taylor was able to work her way up and down the procession and meet everyone. Almost no one wanted to be there. Some would not talk to her at all.

Taylor got a feeling when she was near Viper that he was a bad character. She eased up alongside Brook and said, "Tell me more about Viper."

Brook tried to say some nice things about him but soon ran dry.

Taylor said, "The guy gives me the creeps. There's something bad about him and I need to find out what it is."

Brook said, "Taylor, I think he's dangerous if you cross him. You should leave him alone and just do your job."

Taylor thanked her and moved up and down the line encouraging and complimenting where she could. One girl who never spoke, carried her pack awkwardly, which caused her back to hurt. During a break Taylor adjusted the fit of her pack and adjusted the loading so it carried easily. That won Taylor a smile, but still no words.

An overweight boy they called Porky had trouble keeping up. Taylor fell in next to him and started a conversation.

"I don't like your nickname—do you?"

He gasped, "Would you?"

"No. We could ask Boss to change it."

"No way." A few more steps then, "Everyone would just make fun."

"How about we change it?"

"We can't."

"Let's start with you and me. What would you want your nickname to be if you could pick anything?"

A few more steps and he stopped and looked at her. "Engineer, my dad was an engineer. He could design anything."

Taylor said, "How about you. Can you design things, build things?"

"Yes, I can build most anything."

She picked up a small stick from the ground and, in the manner of a Queen with a sword said, "I Knight thee Engineer."

Smiling broadly, he said, "Thanks, we better get going."

Taylor ruffled his hair as they marched along and said, "Now all we have to do is let them see who you really are. Sometimes people have trouble seeing who we are because they focus on how we look."

"You said you would help people who wanted to work on fitness. Will you help me?"

"Absolutely."

Taylor made her way to two hikers who were walking side by side defying the rule about boys and girls staying apart.

She could tell they liked each other by the occasional bumped shoulder and sly smiles. The path was wide so she walked between them and slowed to their pace.

Without much prompting the kid named Buffy said she was called Stargazer and Jack was called Firebuilder. They told Taylor their stories and why they were at the camp. To them, it was all destiny. Each kid was in a bad family situation that had kept them in constant turmoil. Coming here they had found their love for the outdoors and for each other. They decided to use this time to grow closer as friends and save the romantic stuff for when they could someday be married. They were both seventeen and knew they could wait.

Taylor gave them both a hug as they walked together and moved on up the line.

When they arrived and began setting up camp, Taylor came back from the woods with large bundles of soft pine needles. Taking a shovel she dug up the dirt where her sleeping bag would be, removing stones. She laid down a thick layer of pine needles and rolled out her bag.

Engineer came over and admired her work.

Taylor said, "Time to start revealing your nickname. Since we are to be here about a week, let's build something. Did I mention I'm a bit of an engineer myself?"

Engineer said, "I was thinking, with the climbing gear they have, maybe I could build a zip line. Everyone could enjoy that."

"I think I could work up a fitness program to go with that. First thing tomorrow, we'll see if we can work this into the program."

Within two days most everyone was calling him Engineer.

Taylor got to know all the kids and finally some of them opened up about Viper. Talk among the kids was that Viper was keeping some of the money planned for the program.

Taylor asked, "Why doesn't Boss do something about it?"

Finally the girl who hadn't spoken during the week said, "Viper has some dirt on Boss and holds it over him. Boss is a good man but Viper calls the shots."

At the end of the week, the group made their way back to the original camp. It had been a great week. Many nicknames changed and were more affirming. A truck drove up and Rex and another man came to sit with the adults by a separate fire.

After a private conversation with Taylor, Rex said, "The camp is under new management. In the past five years the camp's success rate has dropped. The finances seem to be, in some cases, misappropriated. Digging into the details, we know who is responsible."

Taylor said, "May I have a private word with Boss?"

They walked to the side and Taylor said, "Boss, Viper has some dirt on you and you seem to have been complicit in allowing him to embezzle money. When we expose him, your secret will come out. Can you live with that?

"It's time it came out anyway. It really was not a big deal. I went to Vegas and ran up a debt. I borrowed some money from the camp funds and Viper found out. Even though I paid it back, he threatened to expose the records. I should have fired him on the spot."

"If you are telling the truth we can work this out. Even though you are a little rough around the edges, you are what most of these kids need. I want to keep you on."

"What do you have to do with all this?"

"I manage things. My latest project is managing this camp and getting it productive, efficient and helping more and more kids. Can I depend on you if we can get this money thing cleared up?"

When they came back to the campfire and were seated, Rex said, "I am the new owner of the camp. Taylor is the manager and chief operating officer. I want this camp to be a shining example of how effective a wilderness camp can be for many troubled kids."

Taylor said, "Viper, you're fired. Agent Bennings has some additional documents to share with you and will be escorting you back to Denver. It seems the Internal Revenue Service among other agencies, frown on people taking money from groups like this and then not paying taxes. Viper ran to his truck and jumped inside.

Annie held up a distributor cap and said, "He's not going anywhere."

Chapter 16

With Camp Backbone-of-the-Devil running smoothly, Taylor scheduled a trip back to Tijuana to check on the clinic operation. On the mountainside high above the clinic, Miguel had been at work for hours on a project that consumed most of his free time.

Struggling to pry a large rock to the side of the path, Miguel froze as he heard a noise behind him. Six men stepped from the underbrush between him and the path back to the clinic. "Senor, are you alone so far away from the hospital?"

Miguel recognized the men as part of a local gang. With nothing to defend himself, he decided to tell them why he was there. He hoped they would hear him out before becoming violent.

"I was raised on this ranch and made many trips up this mountain as a boy. It has always been a place of peace, and a place to be close to God and nature. Now I work at the Cancer Center there in the Valley. What was once my home is now a place where people make one last stand against cancer. The doctors located it here because they believed the scenery out their windows would help to keep their spirits up when the treatments were beating them down. I spend most weekends after working in the clinic, hiking to the top of the mountain. I began clearing this rutted logging road in hopes that someday it would be smooth enough for some patients to walk with me. Making it to the summit and seeing a sunrise or sunset might help them get better. Sometimes a small positive action is enough to make all the difference—enough to tip the scales."

One gang member said, "We have been watching you for a few days. We mean you no harm."

Two men stepped forward and helped him roll the rock from the narrow road. The men turned and disappeared down the trail.

A few days later while working in the clinic and gazing at the mountain from a patient's room, Miguel saw puffs of smoke rise from the trees partway up the mountain. He hurried from the room, asked the doctor to cover for him, and rushed toward the mountain.

Thoughts swirled. *"Was it a forest fire—loggers cutting and stealing timber—some sort of illegal drug operation?"*

As he approached, he heard the rumble of a diesel engine. He saw bull dozer tracks going up the logging trail. The rutted path was now a smooth packed dirt road. Increasing his pace, he rounded a bend and startled the same small group of men. They turned as one, ready to defend themselves.

Miguel said, "What are you doing?"

Immediately relaxed, the leader said, "We decided to help you clear away the rocks. It was much too difficult by hand so we brought along a friend. His wife is one of your patients. We told him why you worked so hard on the road. He wants his wife to have an opportunity to see the sunset from the top."

Miguel couldn't speak. He knelt on the smooth fresh dirt and cried.

"There's more. You must not tell Senorita Taylor. She comes in a few days and Scar has a surprise for her and the clinic."

•••

When Taylor stepped outside the hotel in Tijuana to drive to the clinic, she found an off-road vehicle waiting in front of the hotel. "Taylor" was written in bold letters on cardboard under the wiper. Smiling, she remembered the jeep race she and Scar had when she was last in Mexico. As she circled the Dune Buggy checking out its rugged design, she decided to make a stop at his Cantina to thank him for the ride.

On her way out to the medical center she was followed by a pickup truck. Two men with rifles stood in the truck bed. As she picked up speed, Taylor mused, *"So Professor Wice, you're going to try to capture me in*

Mexico to find the gold and ruby scepter." She could see Scar's Cantina was only about a half mile ahead.

The truck closed in, cut her off, and ran her off the road. She steered into the slide and at the last second floored the gas and flew over the low fence and into the desert. The pickup followed. In a plume of dust, she increased her lead and loved the feel of Scar's off-road machine. Feeling confident she had left the truck behind, she stopped weaving, changed directions, and headed straight for the Cantina. In the distance, coming from the Cantina, Scar was speeding to her rescue. The pickup truck, she thought she had lost, burst from the plume of dust, barreling toward her from the side.

She jerked the wheel when a burning sensation stung her side. Her dune buggy veered hard to the right almost hitting a boulder. As she turned to avoid the collision, another bullet blasted rock fragments near her head. The pursuing truck turned away and escaped into the desert.

Moments later Scar slid to a stop near her vehicle. "Are you alright?"

"Yes, I'm fine. Those guys were shooting at me and got one of my tires."

Unfastening her seat harness and showing her his bloody hand, he said, "They got more than your tire."

She raised her blouse to reveal a three inch bloody gash along her lean side. She thought, *"I hope he notices these tight abs,"* as she twisted to look at the damage. The shallow wound gaped and leaked more blood down her side and into the top of her jeans. Though the pain was just beginning to get bad, she tried to make a joke. "I just got these jeans this week and now look at them," she said, finally wincing from the pain.

"You joke to make light of a serious situation. A bit to the left and you wouldn't be laughing." He came back from his dune buggy carrying a first aid kit. "This will burn a bit," he said as he poured tequila over the bloody gash.

Taylor gritted her teeth and tried not to scream. It didn't work.

Scar told his man in the dune buggy, "Follow the truck across the desert and see where he goes. Stay far enough away to not get caught. I want to know who is operating in my territory. I'll change the tire and get her to the Cantina."

Scar said, "I was watching for you when I saw them run you off the road. Why were they chasing you?"

"On more than one occasion lately people have tried to ambush or capture me. I think it's related to something that happened in Egypt earlier in this year. I've a feeling I know who's behind it but so far I've been unable to prove it."

"I'll capture one of those men and ask him in a way that he will cooperate."

"Please don't do that. I don't want any more violence."

"At the very least I will let them know they can't come into my territory and cause harm to my friends. I have you bandaged up, but maybe you need to have the doctors put in a few stitches."

"It's my first bullet wound. Maybe I'll leave it without stitches. Scars can be attractive."

He fingered the scar across his face. "You do like to play with fire. Good thing I like you."

They drove back to the Cantina and this time, after being shot, Taylor agreed to a drink. She still needed to go to the hospital to meet with the staff and inspect the facility.

Scar asked to see the ruby amulet again. As she handed it to him, he said, "Would this be what the gentleman are looking for who tried to capture you?"

"No. I designed and had this made, but it reminds me of something I saw while in Egypt. That may be what they're looking for."

"And I suspect maybe you know where the object is that they're after."

"I'm not going to respond to that if you don't mind."

"How much is the object worth that they're looking for?"

"What they're looking for needs to be in a museum, but it appears that some grave robbers would rather have the object for themselves. It's worth millions."

"So being the virtuous person you are, you intend to see that it gets put safely in a museum. Is that correct?"

"Yes, that's about the size of it. If it can be located."

"What do you mean by if it can be located?"

"Apparently no one really knows exactly where this object is."

"They seem to think you know where it is."

"Yes, apparently they do think that."

Scar said, "While you're in Mexico I can protect you from the people who are trying to capture you. Once you get out into the world I won't be able to protect you."

"Hopefully I'll be able to locate the item soon and get it into a museum so that they'll stop chasing me. I don't think they'll try to kill me as long as they think I know where it is."

"There are some things worse than death. Torture comes to mind. Do you think they would resort to that?"

Taylor said, "I've had a feeling about the person I suspect is behind all of this. From what I can tell, he's capable of most anything. He and his associates are very shady characters."

Laughing, Scar said, "So I suppose you put me in the category with some of those shady characters?"

"Well you're the best bad guy I know."

With this he held up his Corona and offered a toast.

Scar's man came back from having followed the gunmen in the pickup truck across the desert. He explained where they went and who they reported to.

Chapter 17

While Taylor was with Scar at the Cantina, she said, "I have reports of men spending a lot of time on the mountain behind the clinic. Have you noticed this?"

A sly smile tipped the edge of the scar on his cheek. "I too am aware of the activity. Is your boss Rex concerned about his property?"

"No. But I am. The entire mountain belongs to the clinic so I think we should be aware of any activity on the property."

"Are you implying that I might have illegal activities taking place on the mountain?"

"No. I just figured that a person in touch with all the activities in the region would have heard if something was happening."

•••

Scar escorted Taylor to the building behind the Cantina. It was a long low building filled with tools and equipment. Off-road vehicles and pickup trucks were in various stages of repair.

Taylor said, "You have been holding out on me. I love this place."

"Before, we were talking business. Today we are talking hobbies."

He led her to a newly painted off-road vehicle that had four seats and elaborate seat belt harnesses. The body was low to the ground and it had a small rear engine.

"Want to take a ride?"

"Sure. I've never seen a dune buggy set up like this. The ground clearance is lower than usual and it looks like you have planetary gears on the drive wheels. It's not designed for speed."

They drove the mile down the road toward the clinic and never got over thirty miles per hour. The doctors and Miguel greeted them as they arrived. Miguel walked around the vehicle and admired the design. Noticing the blood and rip on Taylor's shirt, he interrupted the inspection to make sure she was re-bandaged.

Taylor said, "I believe I may be the only one who is in the dark."

Scar said, "Miguel can take it from here. Enjoy the journey."

With that Scar climbed into a jeep with one of his men and disappeared down the dusty road.

Miguel said, "I had a dream to be able to take patients up the mountain if the doctors thought it therapeutic. I worked to try to prepare a trail but was getting nowhere. Scar's men brought in a dozier and the husband of one of our patients did the work on the old logging trail. Would you like to accompany us on the first patient trip up the mountain? We should be able to get there before sunset."

Taylor volunteered to drive. Miguel sat in the front and the patient and her husband were strapped securely in the back seats. The crawler worked perfectly. Like a tractor, it went slowly with no danger of stalling out.

In the mirror, Taylor saw the older couple, holding hands, perfectly content.

At the summit there was a picnic table, chairs, and benches. Taylor positioned the buggy where everyone could see the spectacular view. Even after the sun set, the sky lit up like fire with orange rays bouncing off the distant clouds. Taylor heard the couple in the back quietly crying in each other's arms.

Back at the clinic, Taylor parked the vehicle under a small shed with a sign that read, "Sunset." And just below, "Puesta de sol."

Miguel gave Taylor a ride to the Cantina where her Dune buggy was parked. Taylor went inside and Scar was at his usual booth. He introduced Taylor to his wife who was sitting close beside him.

"How'd the Sunset buggy perform?"

"Perfectly. We really appreciate all you and your men have done. It was a wonderful surprise. These types of situations are difficult. I don't want to insult you by either assuming you did this at no cost to me or insult you by not offering to pay. You know I have the money to pay you, but I have a feeling that's not to be."

"You're welcome. My wife says you have changed me. I think you have maybe hypnotized me with the ruby."

His wife said, "May I see the amulet I have heard so much about?"

Without hesitation, Taylor pulled it from her shirt and presented it for her to hold. She touched it tentatively as if expecting some spark or transfer of power. Holding it closed in her hand she quietly whispered a prayer and opened her hand to return it.

When Taylor first removed the ruby amulet, the gold pendant from the monk fell to the outside of her blouse. As Scar's wife reached to return the amulet, she saw the gold oddly shaped pendant. "What is this one?"

Taylor removed the pendant and handed it to her to inspect. She told the story of the encounter with the monk but didn't give details of how she entered or coaxed the gold bead within reach. She held up the ruby amulet and showed them the gold bead on the inside. As she rolled it over it became apparent for the first time to Scar's wife that the heavy gold cage around the ruby formed a beetle. It surrounded the ruby with body, legs, and pincers.

Sensing her fear, Taylor said, "I assure you these pendants aren't bad or evil. The amulet was fashioned for me from a sketch I did of an artifact from Egypt. The power to change is not in a piece of jewelry. We are sometimes influenced by people, events, things, and a higher power, but the power to change is within each of us."

Taylor put the necklaces on. "I better get back to the hotel. They will be worried about me."

Scar said, "We will drive you back to the hotel and make sure you are safe. I have friends in other countries. Call me if you need help."

Chapter 18

North Carolina, USA

Taylor said to Rex, "Every time I turn around, someone is trying to shoot me or abduct me. We need to get that scepter in a museum before I either get killed or we get put in jail. What do you think about this plan? We make a replica and put it in a museum. Then, once everything dies down, we dig up the original and switch them out. Maybe another museum would want to display the replica."

"How do you propose we create a replica? We hardly had time to look it over. We have no drawings."

"I can draw it exactly." Retrieving a notepad, she began to draw. At times, she closed her eyes to better envision the scepter.

Rex was amazed but said nothing as she kept drawing, even sometimes, with her eyes closed.

"I bet we could get our friend Harry from Harry's Sparkling Treasures to make it. He did a great job on my pendant."

Rex said, "That thing probably weighed six pounds. Do you know how much that gold would cost? And all the rubies, the top one was huge."

"Maybe we could get a fake ruby or, since no one has seen it, a different less expensive stone."

"Harry has all the gold we need at his shop. He's been saving up scrap gold and jewelry for decades. It's part of his retirement plan."

Taylor kept planning and devised an elaborate scheme as she drew.

Rex agreed to Taylor's plan so they mailed the drawing to Harry with a written proposal. Taylor thought about the detailed drawing. *"It sure is nice to get an opportunity to redesign an ancient artifact and bring it up to modern standards. No one will ever notice."*

From the sketches, Harry designed the molds for the casting. Taylor provided pictures from the library of scarab beetles that looked most like the ones on the scepter. Within weeks Harry had molds made and Taylor and Rex went to Huntsville, Alabama to see the gold being cast.

Taylor said, "I'm glad you took a little poetic license with the design. Very few people have ever seen the actual scepter. What you have done is ingenious and saved us a ton of money."

Rex said, "What made you decide to make the caged ruby out of a bunch of small rubies rather than one fifty carat ruby?"

"A single fifty carat weight ruby would have cost millions. The sketch was done in such a way that each facet was bordered by a gold support. They also made the shell of the beetle a grid of shapes so the ruby could be seen through the gold shell. We set the rubies from the mine with heavy strips of gold to create the shape of a massive ruby. The casting will make the handle a solid gold tube wrapped in gold straps. It's really a beautiful piece."

Rex and Taylor watched through the day while Harry worked at the scepter. By evening and, after two rounds of sandwiches, it was done. After the final polish, Harry held it up proudly. It was magnificent!

Taylor was amazed how much it resembled the original. She turned it around and scrutinized it carefully. Without warning she rapped it against the heavy wood work bench.

Everyone gasped.

She inspected it more, turned it again and whacked the bench again.

Rex eased next to her and said, "What are you doing? I have a million dollars invested in this and you are hammering it on a table."

"Remember the dents in the scepter after I clubbed those three grave robbers. Now it looks authentic."

"But no one saw it with the dents but us and Juliet."

"A good detective would know it would be damaged from the fight. I'm just keeping it real."

"Harry, can you age this a few thousand years? The original was tarnished some but still mostly dusty in the crevices after I wiped it down."

He put it in a wood box, added some chemicals in a small tray, added a few drops of a purple liquid and closed the lid. "In an hour it'll age just right."

Two of his children watched intently and took as many notes as Taylor. Harry was turning the business over to them and they were eager to learn all they could while he was still there to teach them.

Taylor had a friend make boxes of rough wood like small shipping containers. They were bigger than the scepter but small enough to easily carry. The top and bottom were screwed in place and the inside was lined with heavy crumpled paper. Harry took some final measurements, weighed the scepter, and handed it to Rex.

"It feels good to deliver the most expensive piece of jewelry I've ever made. Six pounds of gold and a bag full of rubies. I hate to see it leave here. May I take pictures?"

"I would suggest you keep the film and all your notes in a safe until all this is over and the scepter is in a museum. The pictures might come in handy to keep us out of jail someday."

Rex paid him for his gold and the job. The rubies came from the mine and belonged to Rex.

As they gathered the boxes and prepared to leave, Harry said, "How is your pendant withstanding all the wear and tear of everyday use?"

She pulled it from her blouse and held it out for Harry and his kids to see. "Perfectly well. It has been through a lot and is as strong as the day you made it."

"Per your request, no clasp, just welded chain and a heavy cage. Almost like the scepter we just made," said Harry with a knowing smile.

Taylor finished packing the scepter in its custom made crate, and they left for the airport in Huntsville. Rex chartered a private jet to take them to France. He hoped to get the scepter into the country and avoid anyone following them who monitored commercial airports.

An hour into the flight across the Atlantic, Taylor got out the wood boxes. She opened them and admired the contents. While Harry was developing the technique to make the gold scepter, he had poured a trial mold using lead rather than gold. This gave him an opportunity to evaluate the process and make sure the scepter looked right. Taylor asked him to use the lead version and plate it with gold. He finished it out using fake glass rubies and it looked like the real thing. Having perfected the method, he cast another final scepter from solid gold. It was heavier and a bit stronger, but from a distance, no one would know.

Taylor said, "Now I just need to make a little adjustment to my plan to use the fake, fake scepter.

Rex had been following papers written by his university professor. He found that Professor Wice had financial involvement with the Egyptian tomb. The same tomb where they tried to frame Taylor and him for the theft of the sarcophagus. Rex and Taylor were certain that Professor Wice was behind the set up. Rex had done some research and found that Wice lived in a much larger home than a college professor could afford and often was known to buy and sell artifacts from Egypt and other countries. Buyers for his stolen goods came mostly from Asia.

Recently Wice published a paper detailing the wall writings and carvings in the tomb. Though the article didn't mention finding an actual scepter, the tomb writings told of a scepter and the great power given the person holding it during an eclipse.

Rex and Taylor now knew why there was an effort to find the scepter. An eclipse was due to occur in a week. Professor Wice wanted the scepter and its power. They knew thieves would be coming for it.

Taylor's main plan was to catch the crooks and have them go to jail. Her secondary plan was to get the scepter into a safe museum. Somehow she had to dig up the real scepter and get it back on the plane within a week.

She packed and stored the boxes. Rex came back from the cockpit where he had been getting some seat time as the copilot. Already a pilot for small planes and helicopters, Rex learned all he could about flying.

The scheduled refueling in Iceland gave them time to go into town while some weather over the Atlantic calmed. The pilot barely kept the local police away from the plane until Rex and Taylor returned.

Rex said, "What is this all about?"

The officer said, "We have information that you are transporting a stolen artifact. The rightful owners have agreed that if it's returned to them, they will not prosecute you for the theft."

Taylor looked over the crowd to see if she recognized anyone who might be directing the police. There was a dark car on the tarmac close behind the line of Airport Police.

Rex said, "Can you describe the artifact you believe we possess?"

The officer showed a copy of the sketch Juliet had made a year before of the scepter.

Taylor quickly figured that they had copied or photographed Juliet's sketch and either convinced or bribed these officers to hold the plane.

Rex said, "I want to call my lawyer."

The officer said, "You aren't in the United States. The process here is different. It may be a few days before you are given an opportunity to call for anyone. We will search your plane now."

Taylor said, "Officer, we didn't steal anything. We were just trying to get it to a museum so it would be safe. If you can promise me the artifact will go to a museum, I'll turn it over to you. There are people who want to steal it for themselves."

The officer said, "I will see that the artifact gets into the proper hands."

Rex protested, "What are you doing?"

Taylor said, "I can't wait around here for days waiting for lawyers to clear this up. I want to get to Paris and go shopping."

With that she mounted the steps to the plane and came out with a wood box about two feet long. She held it tightly as if she really didn't want to let it go. After a few tugs she finally released it to the officer. Surprised at the weight he almost dropped it. Eyeing the screws in the box top, he looked to Taylor. She went back up the stairs and returned with a screwdriver.

On the hood of the police car, he removed the screws. A big smile came over his face as he saw the first glimmer of gold. He didn't remove it from the box but quickly replaced the top.

"You are free to go."

Taylor said, "Do we get a receipt?"

The officer said, "I can get you a receipt if you accompany me to the police station."

Rex said, "Let's just go."

The engines were turning by the time they were on the plane and they were soon Paris bound.

Rex said, "Great acting back there. How long do you think it'll take them to realize they have a fake scepter?

"They don't have the fake scepter."

"What do you mean?"

"Both our scepters are fakes. I gave them the fake-fake scepter—the one made of lead. And they will probably figure it out when they realize the rubies are fake, and find the note I left them rolled up inside the handle."

Chapter 19

Paris, France

Rex and Taylor decided it would be a good idea to see if they had anyone following them. They spent the day moving around Paris, driving from place to place, being conspicuous to see if they could pick up a tail. Rex arranged for a body guard for Taylor by working with a local agency.

They changed rental cars and drove west to visit the archaeological site, where they had shown Juliet the scepter a year before. When Juliet joined them for dinner in town, they were deliberately quiet about any treasures or the scepter. Conversation was dominated by recent discoveries and additional financing needs. When they knew for sure that they were alone away from the restaurant, Rex asked Juliet if anybody had been inquiring about their visit the year before.

Juliet said, "Not long after you left the site a professor from the University where you attended came by to see me. He asked that his visit be kept quiet and he offered to invest in the archaeological dig. He wanted to know if other people had come to the site and who my other investors were."

"What did you tell him?"

"He sounded a little suspicious so I downplayed your visit."

Rex said, "Professor Wice, who told me about the Egyptian tomb discovery, turns out to be a financial supporter of the archaeologist on site. He never mentioned his involvement. My father dug up the financial connection."

Taylor said, "I met him once and didn't like the man. I had a bad feeling around him."

Juliet said, "I agree with Taylor on that point. He seemed devious to me, too. I even saw him in town a few times over the next few months. One of my employees was seen having lunch with Wice.

When I questioned her about contact with the professor, she denied having lunch with him. She said it must've been someone else."

After dinner, and suspecting that they had been followed, Taylor proposed a plan to try to draw out their enemies. "We should sneak in to Juliet's site at night, pick some random place out in the field, and start digging as if we are trying to dig up the scepter. Anyone watching will try to come get the treasure."

Rex said, "That is far too dangerous. Once they think they know where the scepter is, they might be willing to kill to get it—especially since we tricked them in Iceland. We have a few days to spare. Let's spend it working on the site digging among the artifacts with the rest of the crew. Maybe that will draw them out. If not, we come back one evening and dig as if we are looking for the scepter."

Taylor's bodyguard was with them and had been pretending to be sleeping most of the time. He had really been observing the surrounding area to see if anyone was watching from the road or from the hill tops.

He spotted a few suspicious characters over the course of two days. They decided it was time to dig. That night, after everyone else left the site, Taylor, Rex, and the bodyguard remained behind. The bodyguard acted like he was leaving with someone else but slipped off and hid in a wooded area with his binoculars and waited.

Taylor and Rex made their way far across the field, to draw them into the open. They were nowhere near where they had actually buried the scepter a year before. While resting after digging, Rex noticed two people coming across the field with no lights. As they approached from the darkness one of the figures told them, in broken English, to put up their hands.

Complying, Rex and Taylor made lots of noise, asking questions and shuffling around to create a distraction. Careful not to make anyone trigger-happy, they provide enough diversion for the bodyguard to come up behind the assailants.

The ploy worked. A moment later, one of the assailants fell to the ground. Before the gunman could react, he was grabbed and immobilized. The body guard shined a flashlight on the two intruders. No one recognized them!

Taylor asked, "Who are you and who do you work for?"

They were two young local roughnecks who had been hired to watch them and report to a phone number. They didn't even know what they were watching for. They decided on their own to move in and see if there was anything worth stealing. The gun was not even loaded.

Taylor got the phone number from them and let them go without the gun. She pitched it in the hole and filled it back in.

Chapter 20

It seemed like the perfect time to make their move. They sent the body guard to watch by the car and they hurried to the place where the scepter was buried. Rex looked confused.

Taylor said, "What's the problem?"

"I am not sure exactly where to dig. I thought it would be obvious but after a year the grass and bushes look different."

She had replayed the exact location in her mind a thousand times. He was right, the site did look different but in her mind's eye, there was no doubt. She put hands on his shoulders, turned him to the side and walked him two steps forward.

"Dig just in front of your toes. It's only two feet deep."

Minutes later the shovel hit the bundle of towels that wrapped the artifact. After a quick peek to make sure it was the real deal, they filled in the hole, and jogged back to the tent. They wiped down the tools and put them away. The body guard came to the tent and asked to see what they dug up. Taylor had been around him enough to know he was trustworthy and loyal.

"What we show you is destined for a museum. Showing it to you could put you more in danger. If you still want a look, come over to the table." She unrolled the dirty towels to reveal the scepter. Holding it up to the light, the big ruby dazzled.

He said, "I knew it must be something spectacular for you to risk your lives. It's even more impressive than I imagined."

"Let's get it in a crate and finish the plan," said Taylor.

"You did a remarkable job of duplicating that from memory. The hole in the bottom of the scepter even looks like it'll fit the staff you brought along. You never told me why you brought the staff," said Rex.

"We may not need it, but if we do, I'll tell you then."

Taylor hid the crates in different places among their gear in the van as Rex drove them to the Paris airport. The body guard kept an eye out for trouble from the passenger seat.

He said, "Watch out, don't let that truck block the road."

From a side road ahead, a truck inched into the roadway and stopped. A large car approached from behind and blocked the road completely.

Taylor scrambled in the back of the van and soon reappeared with the scepter mounted on the ancient looking staff. She checked her watch.

"Rex, get out and try to reason with them. Be very insistent but don't get shot. I'll come out if I have to with the scepter. Just follow the plan."

Rex immediately recognized Professor Wice. At his side was an attractive woman. She stepped forward and took control.

"Rex I presume?"

Rex said, "I suppose now I get to meet the brains behind the operation. I always doubted that Wice could mastermind all this. He could barely get the term papers graded."

"Is this your attempt to goad us into blurting out our plans? That only works in the movies. Once you give us the real scepter you can go on your way. We tried this bargain in Iceland and you double crossed us with that fake. I don't have to kill you. By all accounts, the scepter doesn't exist. So, we can hardly have stolen it from you. Miss Taylor, come out of the van and bring the real scepter. I need it right now or I'll shoot your boyfriend. Time is running out."

The body guard came out first and stood protectively in front of Taylor. She emerged from the van dressed in a white gown and holding the staff with the scepter glimmering on top.

The few Hieroglyphics written on the tomb wall hadn't done justice to the beauty of the scepter. Even the fake they got in Iceland didn't glow like this one. Wice's gaze went first toward the blood moon breaking through the scattered clouds as he hurried to get the scepter. His wife caught him by the shirt and pulled him to her side.

"Lay down the scepter and get back in the van," she said.

"I think I'd rather stand here," said Taylor as she widened her stance and reached a hand up to encircle the gold handle of the scepter. She felt the tingle like the feeling she felt when the monk put the gold pendant around her neck. Gazing into the clearing night sky, the moon dimmed as the earth blocked the sun's rays beginning the eclipse. The rubies glowed as if lit with a bulb. The increasing darkness added to the effect.

While the professor and his wife were looking up, the body guard made his move. Running headlong, he tackled both at once. Amid the impact and groans a shot rang out. Rex grabbed Mrs. Wice's arm and kicked the gun away from her hand.

Taylor stood over Mrs. Wice with the staff against her throat. The body guard quickly handcuffed the couple as Taylor eased the staff away. The sky was lighter as the moon shone brightly overhead. Leaning on the staff Taylor said, "I wish the eclipse had lasted longer. I could have used a few more minutes of superpower."

Rex laughed until Taylor collapsed. The staff and scepter clattered to the road.

"Taylor, what happened?" In the moonlight, the black patch spread across her side as blood oozed from the bullet wound.

Ripping open the gown where a bullet entered, Rex quickly assessed the damage. The bullet went in her side and out a few inches back just under her ribs. He packed the wounds with cloth and ripped long strips off the bottom of the gown for bandages. The body guard backed the truck out of the road and moved the car to the side. Quickly dragging the professor and his wife into the back of the van they sped to a hospital.

While in route, the body guard introduced himself to Taylor and the prisoners as he read them their rights. The customs and antiquities officer had agreed to go under cover as a body guard to catch the mastermind behind the grave robbers.

•••

North Carolina, one week later.

Taylor stood looking in the mirror at her two scars. The one from Mexico had healed as a ragged pink line on her right side. The new scars were just under her ribs on the left side. Rex came into the room and said, "Quite the collection. Do you plan on adding to it?"

"No. I quit."

"You what? You can't quit. You're so good. Did someone make you a better offer? I will double it."

"You didn't let me finish. I quit going with you on dangerous adventures, but I want to keep managing your projects. I just have to take care of myself."

"You are in perfect condition. You run like a deer and lift weights and you have better abs than I do."

"You are right about the abs. What I mean is, for my state of mind, I want to focus on things I love that don't involve so much danger and anxiety. I'll continue to be the best project manager you can imagine."

"I may have to cut your pay."

"A minute ago you wanted to double it."

"Just kidding. I accept your new terms. Cut out the danger and bring on the projects."

"And I need time to drive my Corvette and have lots of fun."

"I was talking to my dad and he recommended a company car. He said it would look more professional for you, and I can write off the expense."

"I don't want a company car."

"Well at least come look at it. It's sitting outside. I guess I could just drive it myself."

Taylor stepped outside and was stunned by the reflection off a bright yellow Corvette Maco Shark sports car.

I saw you looking at one of these in one of your car magazines. I don't know a lot about cars so I consulted with an expert. The engine fired up and the dark driver's side window rolled down.

"Dad!" Taylor hugged him through the open window.

"Want to go for a ride, kid?"

At dinner that evening, her dad said, "Your mother and I are so proud of you. You got your education, you have inventions, you have a great job, and you are dating the boss."

"Rex and I are not dating. We tried that and decided we would just be best friends. We have a great working relationship and travel the world together doing good for a lot of people."

"Come to the house and see us soon. Your mom is much better now."

•••

Days later, Rex finally got up the nerve to ask Taylor, "What really happened the night of the eclipse? The scepter glowed and you even seemed to glow while the moon was in eclipse. Did it feel any different? Something magical happened, didn't it?"

"Before putting the fake scepter on the staff, I tried on the real scepter. Don't read too much into this, but I had the same feeling as when the monk passed me the gold pendant. It was like some sort of magic, a tingling through and through. Looking into the scepter I saw myself trapped inside, like the ruby in the gold cage. I put the scepter back in the box and used the fake scepter to step out of the van."

"But it seemed to glow."

"The glow was real. I had Harry leave a cavity in the handle that opened to the bottom of the rubies. Remember, I'm an inventor. The staff connected with the button on the base of a small flashlight I designed inside the scepter. Nothing showed except the glow of the rubies and gold, and the reflection onto my face. I turned it off when the eclipse was over. And then, of course, I got shot."

"I can't believe you didn't tell me about the flashlight in the scepter."

"And I was a bit surprised to find out you had made a deal with the authorities to get me a fake body guard. By the way, what did you do with the million dollar fake scepter after we got the original in the Museum in Cairo?"

"I found a museum here in the States that wanted to feature it in an exhibit. Harry is getting tons of business now that everyone knows he made it. I also made a deal with the Cairo Museum that we can borrow the real scepter occasionally for special events."

"How long until Professor and Mrs. Wice go to trial?"

"Maybe never. They escaped custody with help of an Asian gang and have not been seen since. Most of the artifacts they were charged with having stolen have been spotted in the Asian market. There is some kind of strong connection with that part of the world. My contacts tell me that Wice and his wife may have been employees of someone much more powerful and sinister. The only lead is a single phrase or code word, 3LE appears on several documents."

Epilogue

Rex was right. With Taylor's help, he was able to do tremendous good and keep more money coming in than they were spending. After a year, his father added more money to the account enabling him to help even more people.

They had projects all over the world. Taylor's royalty checks just kept coming in. She kept driving the latest fastest Corvettes and had men all around the world wanting more time with her. When checking on the clinic she made sure to stop at the Cantina to see Scar and his wife.

Taylor seemed to have overcome her memory issues that were related to stress and danger. She still had a phenomenal memory. During the incident with the scepter the night of the eclipse, she had no overwhelming memory issues at all. She thought, *"Could that be anything to do with holding the true scepter during the eclipse?"*

She enjoyed the business side of things so much, she did not miss going in tombs and caves. Leaving the dangerous stuff to others, Taylor found her calling—spending money—getting stuff done—and driving fast cars.

At the Wilderness camp, Boss stopped using the whip to get people's attention. Kids got to choose their own nickname. Engineer lost fifteen pounds and led an exercise group. Buffy and Jack turned eighteen and stayed on for a year working as interns with new kids in the program. They later honeymooned in Breckenridge after Rex hired them to manage one of his properties as live-in hosts.

And remember FiFi the little girl in France? She and Rex made a deal. At thirteen she became the youngest part owner in the mine and her family became financially secure.

While researching archeological news around the world, an article caught Rex's attention. The term Yellow Fever was used as a synonym for gold fever. It referred to man's insatiable desire to find gold. The author compared the death toll of people who annually died of yellow fever in the 1800's compared to the death toll of desperate miners and prospectors of that time. It detailed gold rushes in the United States and made a small reference to some kids in Tennessee who claimed to have recently found gold bars and coins in a cave. *"Yellow Fever"* thought Rex, *"People do act irrational when they get the scent of gold."* Reading the article byline, he placed a call to the magazine editor.

•••

Monks packed their few belongings at the monastery in Tangier. Weeks earlier on the night of the eclipse, the spring that had flowed from the cleft in the rock bluff for centuries, dried up. The monks were told to close the monastery and disperse to other orders about the world. Their centuries-long work was done. Tulku and one other monk were assigned to go to the United States.

•••

With music blaring, the wind in her hair, Taylor dialed her Vette through the winding "Tail of the Dragon," on her way to visit her mom. As often happened, she thought about what the monk had told her. *"Today you are the student. Keep your mind open always. When it is time, open the mind of another like you."* Powering the Vette through the turns, she felt the curved gold pendant move against her chest, and wondered how she would know when to become the teacher.

RodneySylerbooks.com to get free and discounted books

Turn the page for a preview of Yellow Fever, Finding the Treasure Within.

For over a hundred years men and women searched for the lost gold shipment.

Amber and her friends take you with them as they unravel the mystery of a family cave. In a quest for the gold she finds even more valuable ancient treasures, un-matched in the world. Greedy men, companies, and even the government try to steal the treasures.

After being burned badly in a house fire, Amber came away changed. It was this change that prepared her to make the best of her situation, and focus on friendship and helping others. Along the journey she learned about herself, the goodness and evil of mankind, and second chances. She learned people can change for the better.

Come along to 1975 when things were simpler; but hang onto the edge of your reading chair, Amber is not one to let you get too comfortable as she finds the Treasure Within.

About the Artist

Heather Walker is an accomplished artist across multiple mediums. She is a lifelong student of art, and received her B.A. in Visual Communications from Austin Peay State University in 2008, and has since gone on to produce comics, fine art, and commercial photography and video. She can be found publishing more personal works frequently on her Instagram, @its.a.heather.walker. Heather lives in TN, with her artist husband Jarrod, where they both inject art into the world every day.

About the Author

RODNEY SYLER grew up on a farm in Lynchburg, Tennessee, and outdoor adventures were daily events. He enjoyed hunting, fishing, camping, and learning. Young adulthood brought college, gymnastics, racing motorcycles, art, and spelunking. Next, he became a teacher, a distiller, an inventor, and a builder. After nearly forty years working as an engineer, he now adds to the list, writer. He and his wife, Lisa, are longtime residents of middle Tennessee. They have three children, four grandchildren, and enjoy mission work and traveling the world.

Yellow Fever, Finding the Treasure Within

Chapter 1

Burn Center, Nashville, Tennessee

Fourteen-year-old Amber woke up to searing pain and blinding light. A hand went to her forehead and another to her wrist. "Stay calm. You've been through a lot."

"I remember the fire and the smoke. Where's my little brother?" she whispered.

"You've been sedated for a week. You are burned badly across your torso and back. You have extensive skin grafts. It's going to be a long, difficult recovery, but you can do this."

"How's my brother?"

...

Three months later, late spring 1975

Amber's mother shuffled into the hospital room. Lisa had not been in the fire, but her gaunt face and hollow eyes hinted at something equally bad. She brought Amber an old shoebox tied with a bow but instructed her to open it later. Then her mom presented a ragged, stuffed teddy bear. It was ancient and heavy with the weight of sawdust stuffing. Lisa said the little bear had been handed down through generations, and now it was for Amber to pass the valuable heirloom to her children. According to her mother, the box and the bear were her future.

The tattered bear reminded Amber of her own gauze-covered burns. Both the bear and Amber had topaz eyes. Though the bear's eyes sparkled brilliantly, they were no match for the fire of determination in her eyes. Smart and strong, she was ready to get on with life, a better life.

Amber asked, "Why give me this stuff now?"

The other shoe dropped. Her mom said, "Amber, you are strong. I know you are just fourteen, but you are much stronger than me. I can't take this anymore. The drugs, the fire, my son, it's all killing me. I'm leaving tonight for Mexico. You will be okay. I love you so much."

Amber tried to speak, but no words came out. Her mother kissed her goodbye and struggled to the door. In the hallway, she sat in a wheelchair, and a nurse pushed her away.

Lisa had tried to shield Amber from the truth. Terminal cancer forced her to seek last-ditch treatment in Mexico. As the wheelchair disappeared down the hall, Amber wondered if she would ever see her mom again.

Later, her face wet with tears, Amber resolved to get on with her life. She remembered the wrapped box. Inside the shoebox were baby clothes, a tiny hospital armband, notes, and the most recent letter from her grandfather who went by his last name, Preston. The bottom of the shoebox was stacked end to end with bundles of hundred-dollar bills. Amber knew she was on her own when she saw the money. It was time to test her self-confidence. Emboldened, she did an hour of stretching and exercise, showered, and then waited for the physical therapist to take her to the gym for her last session.

Within two weeks, police told Amber her addict stepfather was a suspect in the devastating house fire. Her world was falling apart. Rather than becoming a ward of the state, she put her plan into action. She showed her stepfather the letter from her grandfather, which invited her to come to the farm. Amber told him she was taking a bus to be with Preston for the summer, and maybe forever. She stuffed a backpack with the shoebox, the bear, and the things she had salvaged from the fire. With a few clothes in a travel bag, she made her way to the bus terminal.

It was early summer, late on a perfect afternoon, when the Greyhound lumbered to a stop. She thanked the smiling driver as he dragged her bag from the cargo bay. Amber stepped behind the bus and inhaled deeply. Coughing from the fumes and wiping her watering eyes, she laughed at her mistake. She was looking so forward to the cliché "breath of fresh country air" that she had nearly gagged on diesel fumes. Only later, when she was closer to the farm, did she appreciate the scents of hay and blossoms. She strolled leisurely the remainder of the mile toward her grandfather's farm, enjoying every minute free from the hospital and the city. Skirting the locked driveway gate, she followed the gravel drive.

Amber made herself at home. She crawled into an unlocked window and retrieved her bag from the porch. The house smelled musty and brought back memories of home-cooked meals and Old Spice cologne. After a tour of the house and confirming that Preston had indeed left the farm, she was pleased to see the power was on. Amber finished a candy bar from her backpack and looked around for more food. The remaining food was mostly canned. She saw sugar and flour but nothing perishable. The refrigerator was empty except for ketchup and an opened jar of pickles.

Soon night darkened the room. Amber decided not to use the lights since no one knew she was staying there. After a brief entry in her diary, she undressed, pulled the covers to her chin, and instantly fell asleep in the four-poster bed.

Amber's diary entry: "Free … clean country air … a little scared … I can do this."

Amber was on fire again! She jerked awake to the smell of smoke. As she tore at the covers and rolled to the floor, she expected to feel the heat and the burns. Fear and panic consumed her. She looked around for the flames. Instantly alert, she slipped into her jeans to escape the fire.

It was so dark. She scrambled to the open window to make her escape, only to realize there was but a faint smell of smoke. There was no sign of flames.

Settling down, she took a few deep breaths, removed her hand from her scarred chest, grabbed her flashlight, and toured the house. Everything seemed in order. Nothing was burning.

Amber returned to the unfamiliar bedroom, turned off the flashlight, and gazed into the darkness. It was her first night truly alone and on her own. As she reflected on her long bus ride into the country and arrival at her grandfather's abandoned farm, she noticed a flicker of light in the nearby woods. Could it be a campfire? Had the campfire smell drifted into her room and morphed her dream into a nightmare? It seemed so real. This was the first smoke she had smelled since fire had consumed her bedroom. Almost burning alive in a house fire, made her very sensitive to the smell of smoke. Now she was wide-awake and curious. No one was supposed to be on the farm—not even her.

Slipping into her high-top Converse tennis shoes, Amber decided to investigate. Taking the flashlight and one of her grandfather's walking sticks from a bin by the door, she crept in the direction of the woods. Leaving the flashlight off, Amber's night vision was good enough for her to navigate the yard.

Once through the gate and across the small pasture, she angled toward the tiny flicker. Her feet and legs were wet with dew as she stopped in a rocky creek bed to listen.

Amber tracked the blaze through the trees. The voices were louder as she inched closer, creeping silently in the dew-covered leaves. Amber crouched behind a log and listened. Two boys threw sticks into the fire, making sparks rise high into the treetops. The sparks winked out only to be replaced by the glitter of stars in the clear night. The boys' backs were toward her, but she could make out their profiles as they turned and told their stories. It was apparent they were telling ghost stories from phrases like "headless horseman" and "blood everywhere." Big hand gestures and bobbing motions accented the storyline as the bigger one's long hair bounced about his shoulders. The smaller, bespectacled boy was on the edge of the log, more standing than sitting. Even in the dark, she could sense his fear as he stole glances into the woods.

Amber observed a small tent, sleeping bags, and even an old iron skillet propped near the fire. Concluding they were there for the night, she had a mischievous idea. While she closed her eyes and waited for her night vision to return, one boy said, "Every time you tell that story, you make it seem like a headless horseman is galloping right through our camp."

The other boy said, "That is because the story is true. Headless horsemen show up when the night is clear and there are just enough stars for the horse to see."

Amber carefully slipped back out of the woods. At the small creek, she put down her walking stick and flashlight. Carefully feeling around in the dark, she gathered a half dozen rounded rocks about the size of walnuts. Though yards away from the crackling fire and raucous ghost story, she still moved soundlessly to avoid detection. Amber decided to add a bit of special effects to their ghost stories, like a throw to home base from center field.

She had played softball the summer before and had quite the arm. For three months after the fire, Amber attacked the weights in physical therapy. Having to endure the pain anyway, she embraced it and made the best of the program. She accepted the pain as she stretched the scar tissue and became stronger and in better shape than ever.

Two rocks in quick succession ripped through the leaves ahead of the boys in the darkness. The stories stopped and were replaced by frantic chatter. Since the boys had been looking at the fire, their vision was compromised. They could not have seen Amber if they had looked in her direction. Now, the two boys were standing with their backs toward her. Aiming to the right this time, Amber sent two more rocks into the trees. More cracking branches and loud agitated voices followed as the boys tried to make sense of the noise in the trees.

Deciding the boys were scared enough, she pocketed the last two rocks, retrieved her flashlight, and ducked quietly back across the field to the house. Going inside without any lights, she felt her way along the wall to her bedroom. She took off the damp clothing and climbed back into bed. Content, she drifted off to sleep, thinking the two boys might not sleep at all.

•••

The next morning, the boys were awake early. Their sleep was fitful, waking to every tiny sound of the forest. They added wood to the remnants of the fire and pulled some hot coals to the side for a pan of bacon. Ray dumped two pounds of meat into the skillet and stirred it with a stick.

These were local boys, raised on the farm next door. Because their farm was mostly open fields and row crops, they did their camping on Preston's place. Preston did not mind. The boys had been a big help over the years.

Preston gave them the run of the farm. He asked them to keep an eye on the place while he was gone. They even had a key to the gate and a long string of numbers to call him collect if there was anything suspicious. The boys could hardly believe he had gone all the way to Australia. The female veterinarian he met and ran off with was quite a lady. Once they started going out, nothing else mattered to Preston. He was head over heels.

•••

From the campsite, the aroma drifted over to the farmhouse. The smell of bacon in the morning woke Amber with a smile. Suddenly realizing she had slept late, she slipped out of bed and put on her jean shorts and Converse. Pulling a sweatshirt from the bag, she noticed a wisp of smoke from the woods, but she could not see the tent or the boys.

After thinking about the previous evening, the boys in the woods seemed familiar. Two years ago, she had spent part of the summer planning adventures and playing with them. She remembered one of them had crudely repaired glasses. Though she only saw silhouettes by the campfire, she was quite sure the mysterious campers were Ray and Don Spark.

She went to the kitchen and looked through the cabinets. There were jars of honey, peaches, jelly, and things she did not recognize. She opened a can of peaches, forked out the big pieces, scarfed them down, and drank the juice out of the can. Peaches were good, but she could not forget the aroma of the freshly cooked bacon.

•••

Ray poured grease into another pan and fried some eggs. He stirred a bubbling skillet of gravy. Don grabbed a bag of leftover biscuits from his pack and dished up two plates from the skillets on the fire. After breakfast and scraping out the skillets, Ray brushed the knots out of his shoulder-length hair and stretched his lean body like he was reaching for the treetops. He and Don were having growth spurts, and stretching seemed to make everything feel better.

While Don put away his sleeping bag, Ray went for a walk.

Ray decided to look around and check on Preston's house and barn. When he got to the edge of the woods, he could see a fresh path through the tall grass. Following it to the creek bed, he saw one of Preston's walking sticks on the rocks. He looked back toward the house and had an idea that someone might be meddling with Preston's stuff. That same someone might have messed with them last night! Thinking there could be an intruder; he grabbed the walking stick and made his way back to camp.

Don was getting the camp in order, and Ray explained what he had found. They hatched a plan to find out who was messing with Preston's place.

It could be robbers or bad guys who had been near their camp. Before they alerted the sheriff, they decided to get a closer look. Building the fire bigger to make it look like they were still at the campsite, they slipped through the middle of the woods to the back of the farm. Passing the sharecropper house near the river, they approached the barn and the house unseen.

As they neared the back of the barn, Ray went to the corner and peeked around. There was nothing in sight and no movement. They slipped into the barn loft for a better view.

Don noticed movement in the house. A dark shadow dashed across the kitchen, and Don said, "Ray, there is a burglar in the house. We better go home and call the sheriff."

Ray said, "I want to see the intruder first."

Don and Ray had always been curious. Thinking they might get a better look from the shed, they ducked out of the barn. From behind the tractor, they had a good view through the open kitchen door. Someone was in there. It was a girl. She was looking away, but she was definitely a girl. With shorts and a sweatshirt and dark red hair all puffed out with big curls, she looked really familiar. Don and Ray looked at each other and smiled.

Two years ago, they had met her. In fact, they had spent part of the summer getting into mischief together. Ray and Don had talked about her often. To them, she wasn't Preston's granddaughter; she was a goddess. They had not seen her in two years, but they had fantasized about her and elevated her in their minds to goddess status.

Now here she was, not seventy feet away, light shining across her through the doorway, the edges of her hair like fire in the sunlight. She turned, as if she knew she was being watched and stared right at them. They could not move. Her face broke into a broad smile as she marched straight to them. She remembered who they were and the great fun they had two summers ago.

Amber held out her hand. "Hello, I am Amber Preston. Remember me? I can't believe how you two have grown."

Both boys were speechless. Ray recovered first and said, "You dropped your walking stick." He smirked as he handed her the sturdy hickory staff.

•••

Sitting at the kitchen table, she told them Preston had invited her to spend the summer there. However, she admitted, there was a problem. He had gone to Australia, and if certain people found out she was there alone, they might call Child Protective Services and have her taken away. She explained about her stepfather going to jail and her mother's sudden trip to Mexico.

Neither Ray nor Don spoke.

Amber said, "You are probably wondering how you can help."

After a few seconds of silence, Ray said, "That was exactly what I was wondering."

Amber said, "We could start with some bacon I smelled cooking—if there is any left. I am starved."

The dew had dried, and they trekked across the field to the camp. After bacon, cold biscuits, and three Dr. Peppers, their friendship was renewed. No one had any idea what adventures and challenges would come from this friendship. For the remainder of the summer, they were rarely apart. Even though Don was a year younger, they were all going into the ninth grade. They were fit, smart, precocious, and an exceptional team.

As they laughed and joked around the fire, no one was in a position to see the old truck with a camper creeping past the driveway gate.

Chapter 2

A few days later, Amber heard a truck in the driveway. She knew the gate was locked. The truck drove past the house and backed up to the shed where Preston's tractors and mowers were kept.

Two scruffy men with dirty clothes and beards looked around suspiciously as they positioned two ramps. The men checked to see if either riding mower had a key. Realizing the danger, Amber glanced at all the keys hanging by the door. Next, she guessed, they would be coming into the house. Though it was not quite dark, she waited until they looked toward the house to turn on the porch lights. They took a step back toward the truck. Amber wondered if they would think the lights were on a timer. She did not want them to know a kid was staying alone in the house. It didn't occur to her that being female might be an even bigger problem.

While she waited, she took a picture through the blinds of the men and their truck.

One man made a show of shouting at the house. "Hey, Preston, we're here to get the riding mower for service. Where's the key?"

Amber flipped on the eve lights and moved upstairs for a better view.

The two strangers ran back to the camper, threw the ramps inside, and sped away.

Amber took another picture of the back of the truck as it bounced past.

•••

The driver growled to the passenger, "He said no one was home—and he would buy anything we could haul. I told you he was a double-crossing liar."

"Maybe we need to slip back in here tonight and see if someone is home. There is too much stuff to walk away without being sure. If he doesn't pay us like he said, we will have to make a midnight visit to his big fancy house."

•••

Amber's heart raced. She had a feeling they would be back. When she walked up the driveway to the gate, it was still closed and locked. However, there were tracks to the side where the truck drove around. She decided it was time to make an impression!

The gate blocked the road, and a deep ditch made the creek side impassable. However, on the other side of the gate, the grass was wide enough for the truck to drive around. Amber went back to the shop and turned on the lights. She found some boards in the corner and looked around until she found a hammer and nails.

After driving the long nails through the boards, she flipped the first board over to examine her work. She silently thanked Preston for teaching her to use a hammer. The nail points were about two inches through the boards. Amber made a few more spiked boards and loaded them in the tractor bucket. After locating a shovel, she drove to the entry gate.

The recent rain made the ground soft. By the tractor headlights, she dug just under the grass and flipped the sod over beside the trench. She placed the boards, nails up, in the shallow trenches and replaced the sod carefully to avoid the spikes. In the flickering light, it looked menacing. The next unwanted visitors would be very surprised.

Amber went home satisfied with her work. She crawled into bed, fully clothed. Lying still atop the covers, she was ready in case the scruffy characters in the pickup truck came back.

Amber's diary entry: "Discernment … That is what I need right now … Be brave."

At two in the morning, she woke to a noise on the road. A vehicle passed by the entrance slowly, but it kept going. Moments later, it returned and slowed at the gate. A loud pop sounded as the truck drove onto the spikes. Then a shriek rang out.

A few minutes later, she heard the truck start again and rumble slowly down the street away from the farm. Proud of her night's work, she smiled in the dark and drifted off to sleep.

Amber woke the next morning to sunshine coming through the window. She didn't even know when she had gone to sleep. Maybe the satisfaction of beating the bad guys again had helped her get some rest. She got ready and ate a relaxed breakfast. Belly full, she was anxious to get to the road and see what kind of damage her nails in the board trick had done.

She drove the tractor out to the road, and as expected, there were more tracks. This time, they stopped short. Some of the boards were overturned, and one of the boards looked as if it had been thrown to the side. Amber looked closely and saw blood on the spikes and smears of blood on the board. She realized the nails did not stick in a tire. One of the bad guys must have stepped on the nails and punctured his foot. She decided to take the board with her. The blood sample and the pictures might come in handy someday if she needed to get the sheriff involved.

Amber went back to the shop, parked the tractor, and walked back in the corner where three-sided shelves were built into the wall. She remembered checking for eggs in the nests on the shelves, but now they were adorned with pieces of junk, oilcans, and oily rags.

Pushing all the debris aside, Amber put the bloody board on the top shelf as a souvenir. She remembered her satisfaction from the night she scared Ray and Don by the fire. She fished the two remaining smooth stones out of her pocket and placed them on the shelf with the spiked board. That would be her trophy case—a memory place.

A good feeling spread over her. She did not fully understand the feelings that had started a few months ago. Though the pain of exercising to stretch and develop her injured body was terrible, an internal feeling gradually came to balance and eventually overpower the pain. Now was one of those times. Warmth grew within her, a feeling of pride and accomplishment, like a power she was discovering. It felt so good. At times like this, she almost forgot about the pain of the burns—and she almost forgot about the hurt of being abandoned—but she did not forget the memories of her little brother.

She was startled by a noise behind her. Afraid it might be one of the thieves, she turned with the nail-spiked board in her hand.

Ray stepped back. "Amber, it's me. What are you doing with a weapon?"

A little embarrassed, she put the board back on the shelf.

Ray wanted to know the entire story. When it was over, he said, "Do you think they will be back?"

"I don't know. I don't want to have anything stolen. Before we tell your dad, how can we discourage people from thinking the farm is easy pickings? Let's get with Don, put our heads together, and come up with some ideas."

They met near the cave at the picnic table by the river. It was a perfect early summer day, and the river was almost silent as it drifted past. An occasional sound of someone far away on the river floated through the silence.

From the top of the picnic table, Amber looked up through the trees.

Ray and Don were on the two benches. They understood their great fortune to have such freedom. Some of their friends had to work in the summers. They, too, would eventually get jobs, but for now, they had freedom.

Don wanted to do some hiking in the woods and insisted they plan while they hiked. Everyone agreed and headed into the woods in search of adventure. They talked as they walked, and Ray suggested a game.

They saw a tall hickory sapling, and it reminded him of something he had seen on an old Tarzan movie. "In the movie, natives from the jungle captured some explorers. They pulled down tall treetops with ropes and tied their captives between two trees where they were stretched or pulled apart. They called it Juju."

Amber held up her hands, shook her auburn curls, and said, "Not for me. I've been through enough torture for a lifetime."

Ray explained how his version was different. All three kids would climb the hickory tree until it reached the ground.

Amber said, "How do you know the tree won't break?"

Don said, "Hickory is known to bend really well. As long as there are no limbs, they will bend almost in half."

Ray said, "It will be like a ride at the fair. We bend the tree down, two people let go near the ground—and the other one is launched into the air!"

Don said, "That sounds like fun!"

Amber said, "If I do it, I'm wrapping my legs around the tree so I don't fly off into the sunset.

With the plan in place and everyone willing to try, Ray climbed the tree, closely followed by Amber and Don. As they approached the limbs at about twenty feet, the tree began to bend. They continued a frenzied three-way dialogue as the tree groaned and bent. Soon, all three had toes touching the ground. They looked like clothes hanging on a line. Ray wrapped his legs around the tree trunk and held on like a monkey.

Amber and Don let go on the count of three, and Ray held on tight. The tree accelerated up, and as Ray was pulled skyward, he yelled with delight. He went past the center and swung far to the other side before the tree eventually righted itself.

Ready to take their turns, Amber and Don climbed back to the top of the tree. This time, as the tree bent toward the ground, it was Amber's turn to be Juju. She wrapped her legs around the trunk, and the boys let go. She launched up and over the top as the tree swung past center and then recovered to vertical. Amber was thrilled to be having fun again.

Still high in the tree, Amber said, "Ray, this was a great idea."

Don and Ray shimmied up the tree as Amber was climbing higher to make room. As the tree bent near the ground, Ray and Amber released their grip before Don had his legs around the tree. He catapulted skyward. With his legs hanging down, a squeal sang out as he accelerated right out of his jean shorts. While he swung to the opposite side of the tree, underwear like a white flag, his shorts fluttered down onto the top of a nearby bush. As Don swung back and forth in his underwear, high in the tree, Amber and Ray laughed hysterically.

Amber took out her Instamatic camera and snapped a picture. Shaking the nearby tree and bushes finally brought Don's shorts to the ground. A little embarrassed, Don slid down and retrieved his shorts. He would have been humiliated had it not been so much fun.

Amber said to Ray, "Remind me to put a belt on his Christmas list.

After the Juju, they headed back to the picnic table to eat snacks and make plans. Amber and Ray agreed Don definitely got the most style points for his ride. They decided adventure would need to be a part of everything they did. Making a pact, they agreed to do their best to make life a big series of adventures and to hold each other accountable.